Elle Klass

IN THE MIDST OF THE STORM

TOMMY'S DECEPTION

VOLUME 3 RUTHLESS STORM TRILOGY

I0637744

Volume III Ruthless Storm Trilogy

Copyright © 2016 Elle Klass
Republished 2020 Books by Elle, Inc.
ISBN: 978-0692784006

Books by Elle, Inc.
Published by Books by Elle, Inc.
225 College Dr. #65504
Orange Park, FL 32065
www.elleklass.weebly.com

Author's Disclaimer

All astrological charts are real even though the story and characters are fiction. Whobeda did all charts and interpretations. To learn more please visit her at http://www.valkyrieastrology.com/.

Other books by Elle Klass

As Snow Falls

Ruthless Storm Trilogy
Eye of the Storm Eilida's Tragedy Volume 1
Calm before the Storm Evan's Sins Volume 2
In the Midst of the Storm Tommy's Deception Volume 3

Evan's Girls
Scarlett
Emily
Debbie
Chelsea

Young Adult Series
Baby Girl
The Bloodseekers
hidden journals
Zombie Girl
Realm Walkers

New Adult Fiction
Bone Stars – OUA Short

Volume III Ruthless Storm Trilogy

.

From Volume 2...

2007

July thirteenth: ten days had passed since his grandparents yanked him from Tech camp. His parents' faces flew around him as he followed the familiar trail to his best friend, Mark's, house. He saw his young self, collecting shells on the beach, his mother smiling with his elation over finding a large shark's tooth. The necklace with the tooth on it bobbed against his chest as he walked. At fifteen, he wasn't ready to let go of his parents who were killed in a plane crash on their way home from vacationing in San Diego.

Dillon swiped the pelting rain mixed with tears from his eyes. The winds surrounded him, whipping clumps of leaves and small branches. Oblivious to them, his heart filled with sorrow, he continued on his path toward the beach. Mark's mother dead and his father shacked up with a new girlfriend, he'd understand Dillon's sorrow and offered him an alternate reality as they squashed The Flood in Halo.

He marched up the back steps to his friend's house. The heavy winds and rain pelted his back. He twisted the knob and shut the door behind him. He and Mark had known each other so long they were like brothers. His home, usually a bustle of noise caused by his father's girlfriend's two children, now filled with an eerie silence. Dillon halted, perking his ear to a muffled noise on the far side of the beach home.

Nervous energy simmered inside him as he strolled towards the noise. The closer he got, the louder the noise. Side-stepping the living room, he jaunted faster now, cornering the hallway. His mind focused on the sound emanating from the master bedroom. The door open, he peered inside and gasped, covering his hands over his mouth. His eyes wide as flying saucers. A man thrust himself into the girlfriend, blood curled over the sheets and puddled on the floor beside the bed. The man intent on raping the dying woman didn't notice Dillon, so he eased toward the dresser where a heavy paperweight lay, grabbed it and lunged toward the back of the man's head, hitting him with it. The man fell face first on top of the girlfriend. Unsure what to do next, Dillon rushed out of the house.

Halfway home he realized he still carried the paperweight. He let it drop. Tears streaked across his cheeks. *Is he dead? Did I kill him? Is Mark still alive?* Lost in the thoughts circling his brain, he didn't notice her until he heard a voice ask, "Are you alright?"

He turned towards the voice and looked upon her angelic face for the first time, blond ringlets blowing across it. "I... No. Do you have a phone?" Reality sunk in, he needed to call the police.

"I've already called. I saw it too."

He narrowed his eyes. "Called what in?"

"You're being coy. I watched you run out of the house and drop the paperweight." She pulled her arm from behind her back and uncurled her fingers. The bloody paperweight lying in her palm. "He's not dead and he'll find you if we stand here any longer and talk. Come with me."

She darted across the rain-laden sand, her feet sinking into it, splashing water as they rose again. He chased after the mystery woman. Curiosity consumed him.

Prologue

*H*ow did she know? Who was she? He wondered as he dashed after her, police sirens blaring in the distance. Clumps of dirt and water flying off his feet. A band of rain and wind hit them, yet she continued to run, Dillon on her heels. Tree branches swayed and dropped onto the muddied ground. She finally stopped when they reached a small wooden cabin. It didn't look larger than one room.

Without skipping a beat she pulled a key out of the front pocket of her cream dress and unlocked the door. Once inside, she peeled her mud soaked boots and socks off her feet and stood them by the door. "Take those off," she ordered, pointing to his muddied sneakers.

Dillon didn't hesitate, tugging them off and placing them beside hers. His jeans, covered in mud to his knees, he rolled up, assuming she didn't want the dirt all over the shiny wood floor.

"Thirsty?" she asked, tossing him a bottled water. He was thirsty, but more than that — curious. Catching the bottle, he twisted the top and took a large gulp. The cold water streamed down his throat after the mile or so run against the winds and rain.

She chugged her water then walked past him across the large room and disappeared into another room. When she returned, she carried fresh clothing in her arms. She looked him up and down. "These should fit. You can change in the bathroom." The mysterious woman pointed towards an open doorway.

He didn't care to change his clothes. Instead he wanted answers. Shivers ran over his body from his rain-soaked clothes, so he obliged.

Dillon eyed the room. From the inside, the place looked much larger than it did outside. To the right of the living area was a small kitchenette and two open doorways occupied the wall opposite him. He assumed the one she vanished into was a bedroom and the other a bathroom. Vaulted wooden ceilings gave the cabin the appearance it was even larger.

Walking into the bathroom he, closed the door and peeled off his rain and mud-soaked clothes and pulled on the fresh ones she'd handed him. The gray sweatpants were a little short on his long legs, so he pushed them towards his knees, and the oversized black T fit him snugly. These were not men's clothing, but hers.

He didn't accept her generosity as kindness and thoughts swirled through his head. She could be an accomplice of the guy he smashed on the head. *Was she going to trap him here until the monster he'd injured showed up? Would they hold him prisoner and torture him? Was the man alive?*

When he walked out of the bathroom she was sitting on the couch, one leg curled beneath her, the other hanging over the side of the couch. She'd also changed her clothes.

She stood and padded towards him. "Let me take those. I'll get them washed and dried." She grabbed his bundle of clothes and walked towards the kitchen, sliding open a wood door flush with the wooden walls. He heard the familiar sound of water running and she dropped his clothes inside the machine, then turned to face him.

"Relax, take a seat," she urged.

He met her eyes, one amber and the other green, and in a manner of speaking fell under her spell. Dillon didn't believe in magic, or anything supernatural, but at that moment he considered the option.

Glancing around the room, he didn't see the paperweight. *What did she do with it?* His eyes finally resting on the front door. He could leave and run back to his grandparents. Then it struck him; her fingerprints were all over the paperweight too. *If she turned him in how would she explain that without incriminating herself?* And she'd taken him away from the sirens. If she wanted him caught, why not let them take him? The tension inside him eased slightly.

She strolled past him, taking her place on the plush couch. "If you want to run. The door's there, go," her voice casual.

The part of his brain filled with common sense urged him to leave, but the overwhelming emotional side of his brain told him to stay. Her body language and actions didn't match someone who planned on harming him and he saw no weapons hidden beneath her form-fitting, velvet sweat suit. He faltered, considering his options, then took a few steps closer to the couch.

"Sit." She patted the couch beside her.

"I don't bite and teenagers are a little young for my taste. I'm Scarlett." She half-smiled.

She didn't plan on harming him.
His body eased and he seated himself on
the other side of the couch from her.
"I'm Dillon."

I Remember You

October 2016

Tommy sat inside his truck, the sun slowly setting. Inside the large building, he observed Eilida through his binoculars, her head poured over a book. In the past couple months, he'd studied her habits, memorizing her routine, but hadn't yet found the courage to face her.

When they'd last met before that dreadful day of her accident, which he took in part as his fault. The guilt ate away at him. He needed to make it right but didn't want the door slammed in his face. He was every bit as guilty as anyone else that day.

He'd lived with Evan long enough to know his intentions were not above board, even though he'd never actually seen him in the act. He was a violent man on the inside and calm on the outside. But it was all an act. Evan was a controlling, manipulative, and calculating killer.

Tommy scrolled through his phone, his eyes resting on the map. Until that day, Tommy hadn't wanted to believe Evan was the killer, she insisted he was. His eyes rested on the map as he widened the picture with his fingers, staring at the words *Emily* then *Eilida Tate*.

His body shuddered as he'd figured out too late who Emily was, not only that but he'd helped him! Evan was sick and twisted beyond the worst serial killers in history. He'd given Tommy mail and a package to be delivered to a residence, but never a name.

He dropped his head against the steering wheel in guilt and shame. If Eilida never forgave him, he'd accept it, but merely wanted the opportunity to explain himself and beg for her forgiveness.

At the Astrology conference, he'd taken an instant liking to her and her friend. Sage was far bubblier than Eilida, who carried an air of darkness foreshadowing her. The same evil darkness that ate at him — Evan. He'd destroyed so many lives.

He'd sought Evan's weakness and used it to destroy him, but not before Evan had a chance to eliminate four more lives. Those of his half-sister and her family, leaving only the daughter alive. Tommy tightened his hands into fists until his knuckles turned white.

Releasing the tension in his hands, he grabbed the binoculars and raised them to his eyes. He watched Eilida toss her bag over her shoulder and stroll towards the exit. He started his motor and waited.

The lights overhead blinked on as Eilida looked up from the book she had her head buried in. She glanced toward the window at the darkness creeping over the campus. Checking the time on her phone she sighed and, with one quick movement, closed the book. She picked up her denim bag and stuffed the book inside, pulled out her favorite worn black hoodie and slipped her arms inside it. Then flung the bag over her shoulder as she strolled towards the large double doors of the campus library.

"Goodnight Eilida," called Ms. Rixley, the night librarian. Her soft, round face smiling as she pushed her square-rimmed glasses upwards on the bridge of her nose.

Eilida waved and returned a smile. "Goodnight, Ms. Rixley." She spent so much time studying in the library she considered Ms. Rixley a friend. New to the campus, as she'd only transferred the beginning of the semester, she didn't know too many people yet. She missed Sage to no end and her daydreams drifted towards lusty moments between her and Jay.

Pushing the heavy glass door open, a blast of chilly October North Carolina air swished towards her. She shuddered involuntarily and pushed her hood over her head, tucking her long, wavy dark hair into the collar. With her head down to deflect the wind, she walked towards her car.

Each time she touched the door handle brought back memories of the fateful night her biological parents died. The idea that Evan had been inside the car made her skin crawl, but she refused her parents' insistence on buying her a new one, saying, "A deep cleaning will be fine." Starting the engine, she shifted into drive and left the campus. Within minutes, she pulled her car into a spot outside the apartment building where she lived.

Tapping her fingers on the steering wheel, she decided not to go inside. She'd been studying day and night and wanted a break, needed a break. Leaving her denim bag in the car, she got out and walked towards Flashers. The hot spot all the college kids went to.

She hadn't yet been there even though it was a mere two blocks from her apartment. The blustery wind blew hard against her. *So much for an Indian summer*, she thought. Snuggling her arms around her chest to keep out as much wind as possible, she jaunted the two blocks to *Flashers*.

On the outside, the place was a brick building with a solid neon light donning the bar's name. Inside was loud. Sleek black tables and chairs spotted the floors, while colorful lights flashed overhead. *Pillow Talk* by Zayn played from the speakers. Students filled the dance floor. Spotting an open seat at the bar, she maneuvered through the crowd, dropping her hood and clutching her wallet that contained nothing but her driver's license and debit card.

She climbed onto a black barstool. A young man with thick, dark hair and satin brown eyes turned from behind the bar.

"What can I get you?" he asked. His voice a deep baritone.

"A Heineken."

His eyes swept over her, then he nodded and walked towards the beer cooler. She couldn't help her wandering eyes from watching his jeans move with each stride of his legs. *What a cute ass!* she thought. With her studies, she had no time for a relationship but a booty call — maybe.

He slid the beer towards her and winked as he turned to help the next customer.

Twisting in her seat, she watched the students grinding on the dance floor and felt herself heat up with lust. She'd made a commitment to Jay, but they agreed on a break until she graduated. He was miles away and she needed it more than once a month or so. However, she wanted to stay honest and true to him. He'd been there for her when she needed him, yet her mind envisioned the sexy bartender and her in a passionate moment. *Stop it, Eilida!*

A deep voice and tap on her shoulder brought her back to reality. She turned to see a tall, thin, but muscular young man. His straight, long blond hair pulled back in a ponytail.

"Tommy?" she asked, remembering him vaguely from the astrology convention she and Sage went to. They hung with him quite a bit.

"Eilida, right?"

"That's me," she responded, leaning in close to talk above the loud music.

His pale blue eyes twinkled under the lights. "So, uh, I haven't seen you in here before?"

"This is my first time. I'm finishing my bachelors at the University." She cocked her head playfully. "So, what about you?"

"Taking a few classes. Haven't seen you around campus."

"What's your major? Astrology?" she joked, lifting an eyebrow.

He rolled his eyes. "That shit is pretty cool but no. Right now I'm working on a degree in... criminal justice."

Eilida caught his hesitation but ignored it. "Journalism for me. It's my dream."

The gentleman sitting next to her left the bar and Tommy slid onto the empty stool eying her near-empty beer. "Looks like you need another. My treat."

"A girl can't turn down a free beer."

Tommy and Eilida talked for the next couple hours. She enjoyed talking, thinking of something besides her studies, and was relieved to have a friend she could hang with on occasion. They swapped phone numbers and she excused herself.

"I'll see you around," she said, giving him a quick friend-hug.

He returned the hug. "How did you get here? You need a ride?" he offered.

Enjoying his company and fully trusting him were two different things in Eilida's book. She faced too many nightmares in her life. "No, thanks. I live close." She maneuvered the wild, twenty-something college crowd and pushed the door open, pulling her hoodie over her head.

The cold air chilling her to the bone, she walked swiftly towards her apartment. Her mind cloudy from too many beers. A trail through the woods surrounding her apartment complex opened up to her left. If she stayed the course of the street-lit sidewalk, it'd take her longer to get home than if she took the path through the woods that led almost directly to her door. Her body shivering, she decided to take the chance and cut through the woods. Really, it was just a small chunk of trees with a well-worn path that most people used for walking their dogs.

Halfway through the shortcut, she heard voices talking. She slowed her pace and listened but assumed it was a couple walking their dog.

"What the hell are you doing?!" yelled a male voice.

She jumped and on instinct plastered herself against a large tree and scanned the area. Hoping she was fully camouflaged by the thick trunk. She peeked her head around it and spotted two young men. One had jeans sagging past his buttocks and a red jacket. The other wore all black and he held a glinting silver object. Her mind flashed back to the shining object and black eyes that chased her within her nightmares. She breathed deeply, trying to stay calm, and considered her options. The last time she'd run through woods didn't fare well for her and she ended up in a coma for a week.

Running was out of the question. Going forward was out of the question. She felt the cool metal of the pendant against her chest and remembered its soothing qualities. Taking a deep breath, she crouched, using the trees for cover and squat-walked towards the next tree. She couldn't avoid the piles of leaves littering the ground, but hoped her steps were gentle enough the guys would consider them an animal.

The voices moved closer to her and she went into near panic mode. *Breathe, breathe. They're probably just smoking pot and mean no harm*, she soothed herself, but the feeling in her gut sent shivers of horror flying through her body. Bad memories resurfaced and she saw his face, the monster, Evan's face. She closed her eyes, attempting to gather her courage.

Leaves rustled beneath their pounding footsteps, growing closer with each one. No longer able to control her fear, she took her chances and ran.

"Who's there?" called one of the men, as Eilida sprinted through the woods. Not watching where she was going, she ran smack into broad shoulders and a rock hard abdomen. Waves of horror shuddered throughout her body.

I'm Fine

Eilida pushed the solid chest with her hands but it didn't budge, so she side-stepped to run past but he grabbed her arm. "Eilida."

The familiarity of his voice forced her to look into his face. Blue eyes filled with concern and lowered eyebrows stared back at her. Saved by the pendant, it was without it that tragedy struck. His eyes shifted from her towards Saggy Jeans and All Black. "Did you hurt her? Were you chasing her?" he demanded.

They stood at the mouth of the trail and the street lights illuminated their faces. Saggy Jeans met Tommy's glare. "Nah, she just ran. We didn't know anyone was there."

All Black shifted on both feet. "Really, man. He's tellin' the truth."

Tommy narrowed his eyes. "People don't just run, man."

"Nah, we cool. We didn't do nothing."

Eilida watched her innocent *assailants* squirm as if they really had done something. They were high school-aged boys. All Black took a silver object out of his pocket and grabbed something behind his ear. A cigarette and a Zippo. The moonlight glinted off the lighter and was most likely the object he'd held earlier that had struck morbid fear into every orifice of her being.

Tommy let go of Eilida's arm and moved towards the boys, focusing on All Black who took a drag from the cigarette. "How old are you, punk?"

Sweat bubbled on his forehead and his eyes darted past Tommy as if he was considering whether he could run by him without getting caught. After a moment his gaze met Tommy's. "We don't want no trouble."

Eilida stayed put, observing the show. She knew she should probably say something, but watching them squirm was more fun even with the wind pounding against her back. Tommy stood at least six inches taller than either boy and even though he was thin his shoulders were broad and his chest and arms were well developed. He was like a wall when she ran into him.

Tommy grabbed the cigarette from All Black's hand and dropped it to the ground, grinding it into the dirt. "You're not old enough to smoke." The boy scrunched his nose, then opened his mouth, then shut it as his eyes were drawn towards Tommy's side. Tommy raised his shirt enough for the boys to get a glance at a sheathed knife hanging from his belt. Their eyes grew large as UFOs. Eilida stood on the other side, far enough away, she didn't see it. But the boys did.

"Go, run, before I change my mind," Tommy snarled.

Both boys gulped. Saggy Jeans said, "Yessir," as he jetted across the street. All Black hot on his heels.

Eilida held her hand over her mouth, smothering her chuckle. Tommy glanced at her. "You think it's funny? It was kinda."

She rolled her eyes. "Thanks, I guess I overreacted."

He smoothed his ponytail and stuck his thumbs in his front pockets. "Why don't I finish walking you home?"

She looked into his blue eyes. "Thanks, but I can get home from here." She wasn't sure if she trusted him enough to escort her home. Eilida turned on her heels and took a couple steps, then turned back. Tommy stood in the exact spot watching her.

"How did you know?" she asked. It seemed more than convenient that he just popped up out of nowhere and saved her neck from two delinquents with bad grammar.

"I left *Flashers* a few minutes after you and saw you turn onto this dirt trail. What were you thinking? That could have been worse than two punks."

She twisted her lips. "I live around the corner and walk the trail all the time. People walk their dogs, most of them the size of large rats. It's not scary."

"Then why were you running?"

"Is this twenty questions?" The sparkle in his blue eyes stirred a memory she couldn't quite place. The week she spent in the coma was a week of her life lost, but something about the way he looked at her in that moment carried a memory just beyond her grasp. She flung her arms into the air and sighed. "Walk me home and we'll talk."

He stepped closer to her. "I'm sorry. I can be over protective. But when I saw your face. I saw fear — real fear."

She nodded and took his hand. "I appreciate it. I do."

A motorcycle passed them as she let go of his hand. She jumped at the unexpected sound and Tommy shifted his stance at her reaction, but said nothing. She took a few steps and he strode up beside her.

"About a year and a half ago, I had a bad accident. It took me months to recover; physical therapy every week and counseling. The accident was triggered by something in my past." She hated people feeling sorry for her and hated being the center of attention, so she gave him the condensed version of the story. If he wanted more he could pick up a newspaper.

"Those boys brought back the memory?"

She nodded in agreement. "Something like that."

"I have a few of those too."

She cocked her heads towards him. "I bet we all do."

The brick building housing her apartment was just ahead. Large trees, nearly bald from shedding their leaves, surrounded the entrance. They turned the corner to her apartment complex and she considered whether she should ask him inside — he'd just saved her, in a manner of speaking — or if they should part ways now.

"I lost my best friend in a…" He shifted his lips. "He was murdered. I don't talk about it much, but I get it. That's why I get so over protective. I don't want to lose anyone else, even someone I barely know but whose company I enjoy."

She pondered his words and thought maybe they had enough in

common that possibly he was trustworthy. He'd never given her a reason to doubt it and had plenty of hidden, yet easily accessible, weapons in her apartment. "You want to come in? We can... talk."

Tommy smiled. "We will, but not tonight. I wanted to see you home safe." He pulled her towards him, his firm chest against her, and folded her into a hug. "Goodnight."

She wrapped her arms around him, the heat from his body warming her, then let go. "Goodnight." She turned and unlocked the door.

Tommy watched until she was inside safely, then walked back to *Flashers*.

Eilida pulled her black hoodie over her head and threw it on a wooden table chair. She tossed a bag of popcorn into the microwave and opened a Heineken. Leaning against the Formica counter, she took a swig and thought about the night, about Tommy. The fact that he didn't come inside even when invited impressed her. And she could get really used to his solid chest pressed against her and firm biceps surrounding her.

The microwave beeped and she grabbed the popcorn, padded a couple feet to the living room, stripped to her

24

underwear and snuggled onto the sofa. A fluffy pillow beneath her head and a warm thermal blanket covering her body. Her apartment was a studio. She hadn't wanted to waste money on a place she wasn't living in more than two years and hadn't bothered to hang anything on the white walls.

A picture of her family, including Sage, was propped on the coffee table beside her. She reached past it for the remote and clicked on the TV, then pressed the play button on the DVD player.

Holding her against his body encouraged emotions he wanted to keep hidden. He felt the need to protect her, but at the same time he had a growing attraction. When they first met, he'd ignored it because he needed to be in control. Any emotions and desires for her he'd pushed aside, as they'd have only gotten her killed.

Climbing inside his truck and closing the door, Tommy shuddered from the cold. He slid the heater on full blast and took his phone out of his pocket and typed *I secured the meet.* His finger lingered over the icon a few seconds before he clicked send.

Moments later, a thumbs-up appeared on his phone's screen.

I Hope You Like to Laugh

Tommy stretched his legs below his seat and took his phone out of his pocket. For a week, his mind had been filled with visions of Eilida. Her dark sapphire eyes stained with fear and the way she tucked her unruly dark waves beneath her hoodie.

He'd spent a couple months watching her and knew her schedule and where she was almost every moment. The only way he'd avoided her observant eyes was through hiding. He felt like a stalker. After the night at *Flashers* he couldn't get her out of his mind. Sliding his finger across his phone, he unlocked it and brought up her number. He needed to see her again for himself, not for *her*.

Can I pick you up tonight and take you to dinner? Hoping for the best he pressed the send icon. The only thing else she'd be doing was studying. She'd made no friends yet and spent her extra time at the library. Every Tuesday she did laundry and went grocery shopping. On the weekends, she stayed in her apartment and watched movies or studied. At night, he saw the flashes of light from the TV through her closed curtains.

A message buzzed at him. *Sure, where at, what time?*

Relieved, he smiled at the message then typed, *It's a surprise, dress casual, 6.*

She sent a smiley face. The professor dismissed the class and Tommy stood, grabbed his stuff, and walked several steps down to the floor towards the exit.

"Findley!" called the professor.

Tommy turned and took a few long strides towards him.

"Dr. Ashton."

"This paper," he waved Tommy's term paper in front of him, "this is good work, almost like you were inside the mind of a serial killer. Good stuff, keep up the good work, oh… and… you mind if I keep this long enough to show it to a few of my colleagues?"

His words caught Tommy off guard but he knew there was nothing in that paper to incriminate himself. He shrugged. "Sure."

Dr. Ashton nodded. "I mean it, you've got what it takes and will be an excellent profiler one day."

He nodded in acknowledgement, then turned and left.

He'd said to dress casual, so she had on a comfortable pair of jeans that had garnered only a couple holes and a long-sleeved baby doll-style top. Instead of her favorite black hoodie, she grabbed a purple zip up one. Tommy arrived at six on the dot.

"You're punctual," she said, opening the door.

He smiled, showing straight, white teeth. "I am, sometimes to a fault."

"Really, well, if you're going to hang out with me you should know that I'm not. I'm the person who sets my alarm for an hour before I have to wake up because I know I'll press snooze at least four times."

He shook his head as she closed and locked the door behind her.

The cold wind from a week ago had disappeared, but it was still chilly outside. They walked to his 2016 black

Lexus LX SUV. He beeped the locks then opened the door for her as she climbed inside.

"Nice car for a college kid," she announced, as he climbed into the driver's side, admiring the "new" smell and flashy gadgets on the dashboard. It was like sitting in the cockpit of an airplane and she marveled at the price tag attached to the vehicle. *At least $80,000,* she thought. *His family must be wealthy.* Even her aunt-and-uncle-parents who had boo koos of money didn't own anything this fancy.

"Something like that." He shot a smile her direction.

Inhaling the new car scent. She always loved the plasticky smell of a new vehicle, she said, "You should know I'm not fond of surprises, so what are we doing tonight?"

"One hint. That's all you get." He shot her a quick glance then placed his eyes back on the road.

She narrowed her eyes. "Well?"

He chuckled. "I hope you like to laugh."

"That's it?" she said, play punching him on the shoulder.

The street lights appeared to whiz past them, stretching as they drove.

Tommy turned up the volume on the radio, Adele *Hello* played.

"This is OK, but it's kind of a downer if we're planning on laughing."

"Gotcha." He pressed the next preset and Carrie Underwood's *Before He Cheats* rang through the speakers.

Her face lit up. "OMG! I love her! This is one of my favorites!" She turned up the volume and began singing. Then she cupped her hand over her mouth and mumbled, "I'm sorry. I should have asked before blasting your radio."

Shaking his head, he responded, "It's not loud enough." He pressed the button and increased it more.

She smiled, then went back to singing.

A few minutes later, they pulled into a local comedy club. Inside, several round tables surrounded a small stage. Smoke filled the air leaving a haze, and the walls were painted a dark blue as if the place wasn't dark enough inside. Looking around, she thought with a little love the place could be cozy.

They took a seat at a booth along the wall and a server approached them, her red hair cut short and spritzed to stand out on end, and had large gauged holes in her ears. Tattoos covered most of her body, but she had a sweet, round face and warm eyes. "My name is Triny and I'll be your server tonight." She placed two menus on the table in front of them. "What would you like to drink?"

"A Heineken, please."

"Make that two," replied Tommy.

Triny left and Tommy leaned towards Eilida. "This place doesn't look like much but they have the best food here."

She picked up the menu. "The atmosphere reminds me off my hangout at home," she responded, still ogling the little, dingy dive.

"Where's home?" Tommy asked, sliding the menu to the corner of the table.

"Chesterville. That's where my house is anyways. What about you?" She held up her hand. "Wait, I think I remember. New Mexico, right? And you live with your uncle."

Tommy involuntarily shuddered at the word Uncle. Eilida took notice but said nothing.

"Yup! New Mexico."

"How's your uncle?" She waited to observe his physical response. His shoulder did a slight twitch before he responded.

"He's umm… not so good."

That response didn't match the tension she felt in the air. She should have sensed sorrow not *distaste* at the mention of him. Before she could ask more about his uncle, a man came on stage and announced the first act.

Triny bounced towards their table and placed the beers in front of them. "Ready to order?"

"I'll try the bacon cheeseburger. Oh and can you add extra onions and jalapeños to it?"

"We can," she responded, scribbling it on her pad. "Tommy?"

"My usual?"

Triny winked at Tommy, then picked up the menus. "We'll have it ready in about twenty minutes." She bounced off as if she had springs glued to her feet.

Eilida considered going back to the *Uncle* conversation, but chose to leave it alone. They were out to have fun. "This is a regular place for you, huh?"

They continued their conversation between acts and admired each other during the acts. Eilida kicked herself mentally for being attracted to him. She was a sucker for long hair and great smiles. The way he smoothed his ponytail back and the bulge in his biceps sent chills of desire coursing through her body. Her mind deviated to Jay, then

Tommy, and argued with itself over her growing lust for Tommy.

At the end of the evening, Triny brought the bill. Dillion took out a credit card and laid it inside the black guest book, handed it to Triny, then excused himself to the restroom.

Within a few minutes, the server returned and placed the guest book on the edge of the table, the opening pointing towards Eilida. Her investigative instinct drove her as she peered around the room — no Tommy in sight, she opened the book then closed it. *What am I doing?* She worked extra hard not to be paranoid.

Tommy came back to the table, signed the bill and grabbed his credit card, sliding it back into his wallet. "Are you ready?" he asked, his pearly straight whites smiling at her.

"Yeah."

When they arrived at her apartment building, he walked her to the door. She grabbed the key from her purse and was about to unlock it when he reached his arm towards hers and took her hand. Without saying any words, he brushed the hair from her face and touched his lips against hers in a sensuous kiss. Their tongues swirled together in pleasure. Then he pulled away.

She wanted him to keep going. Men kissed the same way they had sex and that kiss made her juices stir. She could only imagine what might happen in bed.

"Goodnight, Eilida."

Is he trying to be a gentleman, no sex on the first date? Should I ask him in? She'd just considered snooping on him and now, after one kiss, she was weak in the knees and considering how he'd feel in bed. *Get a hold of yourself, Eilida!* She decided to let him make the moves. He was easy going, but seemed like a man who liked to think he was in charge.

"Goodnight, Tommy." She unlocked the door, gave him one more quick glance then shut the door behind her.

The Sleeping Bull Dog

Burkhalder stared at the TV, her mouth shaped in an O. She recognized the name. *Chelsea Mora's body was found by her roommate. She'd come home from practice to find the gory scene in their dorm room. She was stabbed multiple times. James Swan, boyfriend of the deceased, was last seen running from the dormitory. Hours earlier, he'd threatened her publicly.* A picture of a young man with a rectangular face, short, dark hair and brown eyes flashed across the screen. *James Swan is considered armed and dangerous...*

She wasn't concerned about James Swan. She was thinking about the girl. Chelsea Mora was Evan's fourth victim. June 27, 1998, he'd killed her family, leaving her alive but drugged outside the family's burning home. The Moras had kidnapped a young boy, Tyrus, who escaped the house. None of it ever added up, especially the part about Tyrus. According to him, he escaped the house, ran down the road and an older man picked him up and brought him home. The older man and his car were never found.

It got Burkhalder thinking. In the back of her brain, she hadn't let go of the question *Who killed Evan?* Now she thought about it. The bloody scene playing in her mind like a film reel. The style suggested an adult and a victim, or a relative of a victim, who sought vengeance. Why else would someone drug him with his own needle and slash his neck, letting him bleed out? Exactly what he did, minus the rape, but he was naked.

In most cases, drugs were used to subdue a victim when the killer was weaker or smaller. Evan began his murder career at age ten, and the drugs made it easier for him to slaughter his abusive parents. It gave him an edge. Whoever murdered him was merely mimicking his style. The reason she always believed it was a victim, but now she considered another angle. There were signs that Evan had struggled before the drugs took effect. Someone held him down, and that person had to be strong because Evan was built like a semi-truck. *Did he have a protégé?*

Did the killer plan on raping him, but change his mind? Did guilt coat their conscience? And what is the significance of the zircon ring? After spending a lifetime chasing Evan, she understood metaphysical beliefs were what guided him, so she researched the ring's mystical significance. It was considered an Attractor because of its tetragonal structure bringing something new into the wearer's life. Evan's malevolent core in his nature, she liked to think it attracted something as evil as him. The police never released the zircon ring found at the scene.

She lifted herself from the couch, clicked off the TV and went into her office. Sinking into her leather rolling chair she walked it towards a file cabinet and opened the bottom drawer, removing its contents. She never believed Tyrus just escaped. Evan allowed him to live. He wasn't part of the family, so Evan wouldn't have been able to kill him.

Even though Evan O'Conner was one of the most vicious serial killers of all time, he was disciplined and only wanted to kill *his* family. An eight-year-old black boy didn't fit that picture, but did that boy later become his protégé? She sifted through the files until she found it. Opening it up, there was a picture of the boy. She scanned through it until she found his last name.

She wiggled the mouse until the computer screen came to life, then typed in Tyrus Reed. While the computer searched, she dropped onto the floor and sorted through the folders. It was time to solve Evan's murder and she was going to start with the glorious day of his death May 8, 2014.

There wasn't a soul who mourned him, only a country who celebrated. The investigation into his death was half-hearted. There was no evidence, no DNA, or anything left at the scene except the scene itself, which she'd replayed in her mind several times. When she found the killer she might thank them instead of having them arrested.

She made a list of all the players. She was on her way to the Turnwells' when Frank called and she turned her car around. Frank was following Evan, but Evan wasn't alone. A young man was driving the car and they both entered the cabin at Hideaway Lake in Salvation Cove. The young man tall, thin with a blond ponytail — not Tyrus.

Eilida was coming home from her walk and discovered the brutal murders of her neighbors', the Turnwells. She ran scared and crashed down the mountain, ending up in the hospital.

Eilida's car was found near the cabin a couple days later, with a pubic hair of Evan's inside it. That never matched what Burkhader knew happened. It was simply a ploy by whoever killed Evan to pin Evan to his crimes and, combined with Eilida's memories, there was no doubt he was *The Hurricane Killer*. Frank sat outside the cabin waiting on Burkhalder and never saw the young blond man leave, but there was a back door. That's how he escaped without Frank noticing.

Who was the blond man? And how did he get away so quickly? Evan was set up. Did the blond guy do it alone?

She glanced upwards at her computer. It was finished. She jumped up, her eyes scanning the computer. Twenty-six-year-old Tyrus Reed passed the bar exam and took a job in Atlanta working in a small firm as a defense attorney. He's a black belt in karate and worked as an instructor to pay for his college. May 8, 2014, he was in a North Carolina University not far from Salvation Cove where Evan was murdered. The cards were stacking against him.

I Do What I have To

Tommy wiped the sweat from his brow as he continued his usual two miles of cardio on the treadmill. Exercise did three things for him; it occupied his mind, kept him healthy, and offered protection, agility and strength for self-defense. The physical memory of holding Evan down as the drugs pumped through his body made his skin feel like thousands of worms were crawling over it, but it saved the lives of many young women.

The pace of the treadmill slowed to a walk. Tommy grabbed his water bottle and took a long drink, then pulled out his earbuds and tucked them into his pocket. The national news broadcasted on the TV in front of him and a young woman's name scrolled across the bottom, Chelsea Mora. He knew that name from Evan's map. He'd memorized every name and the souvenir that belonged to each girl.

Engrossed in the broadcast, he read the closed captioning. She'd been killed by her boyfriend who was at large. His picture flashed across the screen and he recognized him. Tommy didn't like the guy much because he was always antsy, as if he had spiders crawling up his ass. *Where did you go, James?*

What kind of sick bastard would harm this girl after what she'd been through losing her family? His intestines coiled into a knot and a protective urge surged inside him. Tommy needed to find James Swan. He hurried to the shower and washed the sweat off his body then pulled a T-shirt over his head, pulled up his jeans, sunk his feet into his boots and laced them tight, and rushed out of the gym.

In his Lexus, he grabbed his knife out of the glove box and hooked it onto his jeans. Then he thought of Eilida. She was probably at the college, unless they closed it down. Punching her number, he called her.

"Hey," she answered.

"Are you at the school?"

"No. I'm at home studying. What's up?"

Relieved he let out a sigh. "Turn the news on. A student was murdered in her dorm."

"Murdered," she answered with a quiver in her voice.

"Stay home and don't let anyone inside," he said. He realized the tone in his voice was demanding but he didn't care at the moment and hoped she'd accept his caution until he took care of business.

"I've got the news on. Oh my gosh. I can't believe it. Where are you?"

"I'm on the other side of town. I can come over," he lied. The gym was only down the street from the college.

"Yeah, OK." That response didn't sound reassuring to Tommy and he'd get to her as soon as he could. For now, she was safe inside her apartment.

Tommy didn't know James well, but he remembered seeing him at *The Brown Rabbit*. A small bar about four blocks from the college. The entire bar was no larger than one of Evan's walk-in closets and there were no windows and poor lighting. During a bar fight, someone had thrown a bottle into the only TV, leaving a large spider web across it and breaking the tube so it was always dark inside.

Pulling around the back of the bar, he parked his vehicle, then wrapped his hair into a tight man-bun and pulled *Evan's* black baseball cap over his head and strolled inside. He pushed the tension and anger inside him down and went into *Tommy mode*. Smoke filled the dingy air, making breathing a chore. He rested his arm against the bar and asked for a bottle of Miller Lite. The bar only carried three bottled beers; Miller, Coors and Bud. He wasn't about to drink anything that came from their tap, which he doubted had ever been cleaned. Skimming the patrons at the bar, he didn't see anyone that looked like James Swan.

The large-chested bartender placed the beer on the bar in front of him. "Buck twenty-five," she said in a husky voice.

He smiled and handed her two dollars, then leaned his back against the bar. There were five square tables, all set in a row along the wall opposite of the bar and each was filled since it was happy hour. He took a swig of his beer while scanning the tables.

In the corner sat a young man with a couple other guys. Tommy kept an eye on the kid as he took calculated sips from his beer. Nearly an hour and a half later, the friends left. Tommy took the opportunity to take one of the vacant seats.

"You mind?" he asked, pulling out the chair.

The young man lifted his head and met Tommy's eyes. "Nah, you got a smoke?"

No doubt it was James Swan. Now he needed proof that James was guilty. "No, but I could use a doobie right now." He'd always figured the kid was at least a pothead.

"Man, so could I," he said, nodding his head.

"I tell ya, my girlfriend, I caught her with another man. In my own bed. You believe that shit?" Tommy said, working an angle.

James shook his head. "What's wrong with women today? My girl is crazy. She went freaky on me today. All I did was try and slip a half a roofie in her drink. I was hoping to get a little something that she won't give up. A good T-bone, if you know what I mean." He nudged his elbow at Tommy, whose skin crawled at the contact.

Judging by James' slow speech, he'd been drinking for a while. "How about a shot? My treat."

"Jaeger bomb," he said, lifting his eyebrows.

Tommy ordered four shots and kept James talking. Within the hour, he gained enough info to seal the deal. This sick guy killed her because he attempted to drug her drink so he could plug her in the ass. He had no morals and was a waste of taxpayer time and money.

Tommy had a better solution. "I think I know where we can get a bag. You in?"

A couple hours later, Tommy showed at Eilida's. She didn't hesitate to let him inside and relished the fresh shower scent on his body and damp hair.

"Sorry I'm late. I stopped at home and freshened up," he said as he lifted a bag, "also got us dinner. I hope you didn't eat yet."

"Yummy!" She closed the door behind him. "Put that on the table. I'll get us plates."

He watched her round ass sway gently as she padded to the kitchen. Her shirt rose, exposing the small of her back as she reached for the dishes. He shook his head and opened the bag, lifting two containers out of it. "Chicken or steak?"

She set the plates on the table. "A little of each," she smiled.

With their loaded plates, they took a seat on the sofa.

"The police are still searching for that guy, James Swan," said Eilida.

Tommy heard the sadness in her voice. "Guys like that get what's coming to them," he responded. James' panic when he eyed Tommy's knife buzzed through his head and a tiny smile played on his lips.

Eilida, gazing at the blank TV screen for a second, missed Tommy's facial expression. She responded, "I guess, eventually. In the meantime, they are asking students to be vigilant. You know, stay in pairs, watch each other's backs and they canceled classes tomorrow."

He knew she was thinking about Evan and all the families he destroyed, including hers, before he received his punishment. James Swan wouldn't be hurting anyone again.

He wanted to make all the bad in her life disappear and he wanted her. The vibes bouncing off Eilida suggested she desired him just as much. Setting his plate on the table, he turned to face her and cupped her face in his hand. Then he brought his lips to hers. His sexual hunger matched by hers.

When they released the kiss, she set her plate beside his and brought her body closer to his, melting in his arms. Their mouths met again as their hands explored the other's assets. His hand lingering on her perky breasts as he lifted her shirt and drew his tongue closer to them for a taste.

Her small hand rubbed against his throbbing hard-on and a small gasp of pleasure escaped her mouth. He wasn't sure if it was from his size, or pleasure as he gently nibbled on her breasts. She fought against the button and zipper of his jeans as her hand dove inside, clutching his hardness.

Sinking onto the sofa together, they undressed each other and tossed clothes randomly across her floor. Soon, their naked, ravenous bodies entwined as he thrust inside her. The walls of her vagina squeezing him and driving his desire for her until they both collapsed moaning in ecstasy.

Ghosts of Family Past

The Next Day

Her blond hair spilled over the back of the lounge chair and the pool water sparkled in the sun. She lifted her arm and tossed her tresses above her head to cool off in the heat.

"How is everything, darling?" she cooed.

"It's going," said a male voice on the other line.

"You don't sound too excited. I know you, and this is something we both want."

She heard the unmistakable sound of a sigh and hesitation. "I'm busy."

"Not just with school. Tell me about her!" She always had a difficult time containing excitement.

"She's cool. But... I don't know, maybe we should leave her out of this." She heard the skepticism in his voice.

She took a sip of her Bloody Mary and placed it back on the glass top table beside her. "Second thoughts. Have I ever steered you wrong?"

"No, but… she's been through a lot of trauma and may not be ready."

She shook her head. He took everything to heart. Never a light moment with him. She glanced upwards at the master bedroom window and saw a shadow – Philmonia's. Used to the ghosts that roamed Poppy Hills she dismissed her sister and set her phone on the table then pressed the speaker icon and applied sunscreen to her legs. "It's about closure, for her. She needs us."

"She jumps at the slightest sound," Tommy said, remembering how Eilida sprang as the motorcycle passed them.

"Listen to me, honey. I used to be her; trauma, drama, nightmares, all of it. Now I sleep easy even with their ghosts watching my every move." She glanced at the window again and Philmonia was gone. "You like this girl, get over your protective papa bear attitude and reel her in. She needs this." She emphasized *she needs this*.

"I think we need her more."

"Nonsense! She wants to be an investigative reporter. We are handing her the biggest story of her life!"

"It is her life!" His will to protect came out stronger than expected.

"Yes, you're right. And my life, and yours, and hundreds of other people." She put her finger up and scolded the air as if he could see her. "You like this girl and I'm not talking friendship. You're in love."

"I'm not arguing about this. I'm here, you're there. If you think you can do this better then get your ass off the pool chair and join me in the cold. We can switch places!"

Sensing his anger, and knowing she could only push him so far, she backed off and changed the subject. "Are you visiting for Thanksgiving?"

"I'll think about it." Then the phone went dead.

"Damn that boy!" she hollered into the air. Sliding her flip-flops from under her chair, she slipped her feet into them and padded to the kitchen to refill her drink.

Tommy slammed his phone onto the counter, cracking the case. His thoughts filled with Eilida. Then Evan swam into view, his dark eyes reaching into his soul from beyond the grave. If he felt this way, how did Eilida feel? He hated to admit that maybe she was right.

The night he met her. The circumstances fluttered through his mind. Candlelight bounced against the walls of the small cabin and the storm cleared.

She candidly told him her story. One that easily could be written into a horror novel. "He was born of evil intentions and will always be… evil."

The back of the man's head he crashed the heavy paperweight against flashed through his mind. He hadn't only killed her but was raping her corpse. He cringed at the memory still very fresh in his head.

"He must be destroyed," she said in a chilling voice, her expression one of determination.

As much as he wanted to annihilate the man who took his friend's life. *How could he be sure they were the same man?* He shifted his eyes away from her penetrating gaze and stared blankly at the light dancing against the wooden wall.

"You question whether it's the same guy. It's him. Do you want me to show you?"

Show me? "How are you going to do that?" A childish question with a response he didn't expect.

Scarlett lifted herself off the couch and strolled into the kitchen. Dillon contorted his body to watch her movements. She stood on her tiptoes and pulled a small, empty, purple-flowered vase from above the dryer and dumped it over. A small object landing in her palm. She turned on her heel and he quickly resumed his position so she wouldn't know he'd been watching.

She grabbed her cell phone and took the back off, sliding the object, an SD card, into a slot then positioned the back onto the phone and turned it on. Dillon sat still and silent as he watched.

Turning towards him, she held the phone in front of him. He gulped, his eyes wide as he lifted his hand palm out, then curled his fingers making a fist. He didn't think she could actually prove it but now that her proof was in front of him it brought the fear he'd felt when he first saw the bloody room and witnessed… he didn't want to think about it. His stomach churned as he pushed away the recent memory.

"Here," she shoved it towards him, "it won't bite."

He unfisted his hand and grabbed the phone, but didn't yet look at the screen.

"Just click here," she pointed to a button, "and it will move to the next screen."

Gulping, he shifted his eyes to the picture staring at him. A man with a bald head and baby blue eyes that seemed to shift like in a creepy picture in a haunted mansion. The next picture was the same man. They were all taken from different angles. His heart knocked against his chest and he squeezed his eyes closed, not wanting to see any more, but the man's ugly face burned inside Dillon's mind.

Opening his eyes wide, he tossed the phone back at her. "Why do you have all those?"

"There's more. You need to see them."

He didn't want to, not today, not ever. Dillon shook his head. "I need to get home."

She nodded, slipped the SD card out of the phone and dropped it into its hiding spot, a place it should stay. Plucking a set of keys from a small table behind her, she walked towards the door.

"I can walk." He wasn't sure if he wanted to see her ever again, even though his mind raced with curiosity.

"It's better I drive you. The storm is over but it's dark and there's plenty of debris on the ground to trip you."

She hadn't thought of the debris littering the ground when she brought him to the cabin. The day was worse than any nightmare he'd ever had and he was tired. Instead of arguing he said, "I need to change." Her clothes still hugging his body.

She nodded confirmation as she turned then strolled towards the dryer, lifting his clothes and bundling them in her arms.

"Thanks," he said, grabbing the bundle and heading towards the bathroom to change. He didn't know yet what to think of her and wanted home, but not the one with his grandparents. No, he wanted home with his parents. Dillon fought the tears escaping his eyes and wiped a hand across the bottom of his nose as it grew hot from tears and began running.

She followed behind him as he exited the cabin. Dillon halted midstride, then turned towards her. "It wasn't a coincidence you finding me in the woods."

She smiled. "Not exactly. When you're ready, I have more to show you."

That's what he was afraid of —
more.

Finals

Eilida put on her headphones and listened again to her final project in journalism. They were to write an article on a true crime. Their interviews could be, but not limited to, police who worked the case, journalists, and anyone mentioned in the police reports.

She tapped her fingers against her knee which rested on her other leg. An unsolved crime. Her life was an unsolved true crime. She stood, hefted her bag over her shoulder and walked to Ms. Rixley's empty desk. Within a few minutes, she returned and offered Eilida a warm smile.

"What can I help you with today?"

Eilida leaned against the counter separating them. "Do we have microfilm on crimes in the state of North Carolina?"

"Oh yes!" she said, as if it excited her. "This college having such large criminal justice and journalism departments we have reels that date back to the early '30s. Follow me." Ms. Rixley opened the swinging gate and walked to

Eilida's side of the counter. Her dress swished with her large hips as she guided Eilida to the viewers.

Eilida followed.

"What year are you looking for?" she asked, opening a large cabinet that contained dated reels of microfilm.

Eilida thought about the question. She had solved, with the onslaught of her own repressed memories, her family's murders. *Evan O'Conner.* The psychopathic guilty party. But the mystery remained who killed him. His bloody body found in a motel room after his throat had been slit. Much in the same fashion he'd done his victims. The images of her family surfaced and she shuddered.

His death had been a hot topic for a couple months then went cold — dead cold. She really didn't care who killed him, only that he was dead. Yet, it nagged at her. *Who killed him? Would solving the crime give her closure, or put one of his victims on the hot plate?*

She decided if it came down to it, she would keep the killer's identity out of the limelight unless the killer was as cold-blooded and psychotic as Evan. That's if she solved the crime. "May 8, 2014, in Salvation Cove."

Ms. Rixley's eyes popped open and she adjusted her square-rimmed glasses with the mention of the town. 'That's recent. I remember the man's face all over the papers." She leaned in as if it was a secret. "Things like murder don't happen in Salvation Cove. Are you sure you want to read about that one?"

Eilida knew what she was getting at. His murder had been gory, but it was unsolved and fit the bill for her assignment, and maybe she'd be able to thank Evan's killer. She smiled at the thought, then wondered if his killer was as insane as he. Goosebumps pimpled her arms and her smile disappeared. "Yes. That's the one."

"Well, O... K... if you insist." She pulled out a few reels of microfilm and showed Eilida how to use the machine.

"Thank you," Eilida said with a slight tremor in her voice. Rehashing her fears wasn't a top priority, but she needed to know and test her own journalistic skills. She tricked herself into believing if she solved this it would help make sense of the needless deaths and torture the monster, Evan, had caused in his lifetime.

Ms. Rixley nodded. "If you need anything, I'm closing tonight."

Eilida shot her a halfcocked smile, then took a deep breath as she began scanning the reels of film.

A few hours later, with Zerox copies, tedious notes, and plenty of info on the vile man whose death remained unsolved, she returned home. Her phone buzzed and she checked it; a text from Tommy. Can you come over? *I'll cook us dinner.*

What time? And address.

Soon as you're ready. And his address popped up on her screen.

It struck her that she hadn't been to his home, but he'd been to hers a few times. Eilida stuck the key in her door and turned. When she didn't hear the familiar click, she pushed the door. It creaked open. The hairs on her arms stood on end as she contemplated whether she should enter the apartment. She thought back to when she left earlier and remembered locking her door. She always did, out of paranoia.

After reading and following what was known of the monster's life, the notes stuffed into her backpack, she was edgier than usual and fish did flip-flops in her belly.

She took a couple steps to the threshold and turned the light on. With James Swan still on the loose and growing up on a diet of PTSD, fear, nightmares and horror movies, she knew better than to enter without a light or chase strange noises — which left her still standing in the doorway, shivering from a mix of fear and cold, fall air. A rustle from the bushes beside her house caught her attention and her heart hammered against her chest.

When the little poodle across the hall rounded the corner with his owners on the other side of the leash, she let out a long sigh.

Her neighbors, who she'd seen but never had deep discussions with, stopped. They were a fortyish couple. "Are you alright?" asked the woman. A short web of lines reached from the corners of her eyes.

Eilida thought quickly. Her options were to run to Tommy or go into her apartment. She wasn't going alone. "I saw something slither along the wall into my bathroom. I think there's a snake."

The man shook his head. "It's too cold outside for them. They're in hibernation. Are you sure it was a snake?"

"Not 100 %, but I'd feel better if someone went inside with me. I have a couple things to grab and I'll call the office first thing tomorrow."

The man placed his hands on his jean-covered hips. "I'll go in with you." He looked towards the woman. "Jule, you stay here. If it's a snake, you'll cause more problems than you'll help."

She nodded. "I hate those things. Just kill it. We don't want it sneaking into our apartment." She visibly trembled for a few seconds.

"It's probably not a snake, but let me take a look." He entered the apartment before Eilida and walked around the edges of the large room, peeking behind furniture, then walked into the bathroom.

Eilida gathered a handful of clothes and stuffed them into her denim bag, which was already filled with her project research. She looked around. Nothing appeared out of place.

The neighbor walked out of her bathroom. "No snake, but you need to be more careful about leaving your windows open."

She hadn't left her window open. Eilida took care to double check her windows and doors each night before going to bed, and again in the morning before leaving. There was no way she'd left it open. "I don't remember leaving it open, must have been steamy from my shower."

He nodded. "I closed it."

"Thanks," she said as they walked toward the front door.

"No problem. You have a good night," he said, closing the door.

"No need to close that, I'm leaving in a second." With the door open, her neighbors would hear her better if she screamed for help...

He nodded.

He just left here, get it together, she thought. Edging toward the bathroom with caution, she jumped into the room and grabbed her toothbrush with haste, then reappeared in the living room. Her heartbeat slowing a couple notches.

Eilida opened the cabinet beneath the kitchen sink and pulled out a large twenty-ounce hammer. She glanced toward her nightstand a few paces away and scurried towards it, reaching under and pulling out a solid, pointy, and thoroughly heavy trowel with a long handle. She stuffed both objects into her bag and left, locking the door behind her.

Thrusting the bag over her shoulder, she dashed to her car. The parking lot was well-lit and she saw no movement in or around her car. She beeped the lock, hoisted her bag onto the passenger seat and jumped into her car, immediately clicking the locks. She ran her hand beneath her seat and felt the large, cylindrical, police-fashion night-stick. It was a gift from Burkhalder. Blowing out a deep, nervous breath, she started the car and reversed.

She spoke Tommy's address to the map app on her phone. It told her to turn left. A minute or so later, another car made a left from the apartment complex she lived. It wasn't uncommon, and someone could be heading the same way, she told herself in order to calm down. With one hand on the wheel, she clutched her pendant with the other.

Traffic was light, so it didn't take much effort for her to keep an eye on the other car. It stayed a few car links behind her, making each turn she did. A tsunami of anxiety cropped inside her.

About an hour later, her car pulled up beside Tommy's Lexus in the driveway. She exited it, then scuttled around the passenger side and yanked out her denim bag stuffed to the hilt. She heaved it over her shoulder and he wondered what was in it. Clothes certainly wouldn't be heavy enough by themselves. She dashed towards his door. Eilida's behavior was strange even for her. He opened the door and walked towards her, reaching for the bag.

"No, I got it," she said, her voice quivering as she nearly ran him over to get inside.

He pushed the door closed and she demanded, "Lock it."

The thought of being locked alone with her anywhere caused a flurry of lust-filled thoughts to wash over him, but her tone and actions sent them packing. "What's going on?"

Eilida curled onto his cream, velvety couch, her denim bag over her lap. "There was someone in my apartment."

His eyes widened. "Are you sure?"

"Yes. The front door was unlocked and whoever it was escaped out the bathroom window. Then a car followed me. I think I took enough turns that I finally lost him or her." She stared at him. Her orbs of sapphire nearly covered by the black of her pupils. "It could be that James guy."

It definitely wasn't James. "I wished you'd have called me," he said, taking a seat beside her.

"What could you have done? You weren't with me. If I followed this route direct to your house, it's ten minutes from mine. I could be dead in that time."

He felt her body tremble as he reached his arm around her and pulled her closer. Everything was working out better than he planned. Now that Evan was dead, there was no one who wanted to harm her. But if she obsessed on James Swan, he'd use it to his advantage.

Another thought entered his head. *She* wanted them closer. Complained he wasn't working fast enough. If *her* plan was to drive Eilida to him, it worked, but he didn't like the price. And it wasn't really *her new style* since she started living the good life in New Mexico. A flight to North Carolina to scare Eilida didn't fit her personality. Then again, it fit her past life to a perfect T and he'd dared her to come here and do better. *Damn!*

"Was anything missing?" he questioned.

"No. Nothing I saw looked out of place." She nuzzled her head against his shoulder.

He loved having her close and running to him for safety, but not like this. Several nasty words filtered through his head as he fought to control his anger. "I'm going to your apartment in the morning."

She lifted her chin and their eyes met. Next their lips found each other. She pulled herself over and straddled him. The rage inside him dwindled as their mouths were all over the other. He nibbled the lobe of her ear while she grinded on top of him. He felt her wetness through their jeans and his cock throbbed and yearned for her. Flipping her so her back was on the couch, he pulled her pants off and skimmed his tongue across her pussycat, tickling her clit.

Moving up her body he savored the softness of her skin as he dropped kisses, working his way to her breasts and swirling his tongue around her nipples. She grasped his hair then worked her hands across his back, sliding them over his abs and finally manipulating the button of his jeans.

He helped push them down, then kicked them across the room, and she worked his shaft that throbbed with wanton heat and hardness.

If she didn't drive him wild, he'd kick himself for his lack of control around her. All she had to do was look at him and his cock saluted like a private. Add touching and kisses and it grew larger and harder than he'd thought possible and he had to have her.

Sliding in and out, she squeezed against him and it took everything he had to keep going and not erupt. She grasped his ass and held him tight as if she wanted him deeper inside her. He thrust his hips against her and she rotated hers. Small, than larger, moans escaped her lips and he knew if he could control his ejaculation for just a few more thrusts she'd complete her orgasm. But, as she tightened around him, his cock had other ideas. He roared with pleasure while he exploded inside her.

At that moment, she screamed and ran her nails across his back. Satisfaction spread across his face as he'd given her just enough time to reach her climax.

Sunlight streamed through the cracked curtains and it took her eyes a minute to adjust to the surroundings and her mind a minute to remember she was in Tommy's house. He lay beside her, sleeping soundly.

Her phone on the nightstand blinked, informing her she had a message. She crept out of Tommy's bed. Grabbing a blanket, she wrapped her naked body and sauntered down the stairs. Tommy's wallet lay on the kitchen table. She'd stopped herself from spying on his credit card but, fear still rising in her belly from her experience yesterday, she edged closer to the table and flipped it open. Investigating was her nature and she knew little about him, yet had slept with him two nights in a row. The top of his driver's license peeked out of a pocket. She peered around to make sure he wasn't coming down the stairs, then slid it out.

She felt guilty as hell, but her experiences in life beckoned her to be cautious. Over the past few days, she and Tommy had spent a lot of time together and now here she was in his house. She spent the night and they barely knew each other.

The name *Dillon Thomas Findley* was printed on his ID. Her brain chattering *Thomas is his middle name, a lot of people go by their middle names.* Her eyes scanned further and his birthday sent chills raining down her back - June 30, 1992. She clutched the pendant around her neck and allowed its soothing energy to take over her.

'The center stone is moonstone, an excellent Guardian, and the smaller stones are kyanite, a traditional Barrier,' she remembered the man's words when he sold her the pendant. Smoothing the center stone with her fingers, its energy calmed her. She inhaled a few deep breaths.

In control of her fear, she thought rationally. *It's not his fault he was born the same night as Hurricane Chloe.* The night her parents and brothers were viciously taken from her. Eilida had watched in horror the night her family was murdered in front of her as she hid behind her mother's dresses in the closet on June 30, 1992. Evan O'Conner slaughtered her family in cold blood before her innocent eyes. The same night Dillon was born.

It can't be coincidence that we meet again, here. Eilida believed in a lot of things, but this was too much. She flashed back to the astrology convention and Patrice Renard's words filled her head as she interpreted her natal chart. *We call this blue triangle a yod or the finger of god.'*

'What does it mean?'

'A fated life, but let's get through all of it before you decide what that means. This blue line ties Pluto in the 3rd house to the Sun in the eighth house. This implies that you crave powerful experiences and are attracted to the unfathomable.'

The unfathomable, that's what this is. Patrice! She left me her card. Dumping her purse out and emptying her wallet, she shuffled through every card until she found it. She grabbed her phone and dialed the number. It rang a few times then went to voice mail. She left a quick message and her number.

Picking her tablet back up, she Googled newspaper articles from that date, hoping to find something about Tommy. A disturbing sensation tingled her gut. On the second search page, she found it with a picture of his parents. His mom holding him, cradled in her arms. They made the front page. She scribbled a few notes on a random piece of paper lying on the end table. *Dillion Thomas Findley born at 9 p.m.…. Detective Burkhalder and Deputy Martin led them to safety… Burkhalder, how much does she know?* After she talked with Patrice, maybe she'd give

Burkhalder a call. He was the "miracle" baby born during Hurricane Chloe.

He was born the day her family was slaughtered. Was it coincidence? It couldn't be possible. Billows Hollow was a small blip on the map. A tiny island on North Carolina's outer banks. She knew she had to suck up her fear and confront him. The scars left on her heart and soul were a battle, but she intended to make it an uphill battle, ending with closure.

It didn't say anything negative about him. He wasn't in charge of his birthday, but she found it odd this day connected them. Maybe that was the chemistry between them. The little voice inside her head chattered away and she needed to know more about him. *If I ask, will he be honest? What does he know about me?* She slid his license back into its pocket and folded his wallet so it appeared undisturbed. Her heart pumped faster than usual and blood flowed in heavy rivers through her veins, chased by the demon of her past. *Calm down, breathe.*

Mind spinning, Eilida's thoughts returned to her phone. Creaking open the door leading to his townhome's small deck, she took a seat and read Jay's text. He wanted to know if she'd be visiting for Thanksgiving — only a week and a half away. Wrapping the blanket tighter around her middle to fight the cold, she returned Jay's call.

"Hello," answered a groggy Jay.

"Hey."

"E? You never call this early. Is everything OK?" The concern in his voice spanned the airways between them.

"Yeah, I miss you." A slight guilt crept into her heart and she worked to cover it in her voice. She missed the heck out of him, but had too many things on her end to investigate. Like her final project and *Dillon Thomas Findley.*

"Are you sure you're OK?"

A movement of brown caught the corner of her eye and she jumped, her eyes moving towards it. A squirrel, it's only a squirrel. Focusing back on Jay, she knew he worried about her daily. "I am. More than good. Listen I… I won't be coming home for Thanksgiving."

"Why not?" She heard the unmistakable hurt in his voice.

"I have this huge term paper due for my journalism class and need the time to work on it." *And I need to find out more about Tommy,* she kept that to herself.

"Do you need me there? I can take the time." She heard the longing in his voice but couldn't very well have him here and snoop on Tommy at the same time. *You don't want him here so you can fuck Tommy freely*, her mind jested.

"No, I'll be home for Christmas," she assured him. The door behind her creaked open and Tommy took a seat next to her. Her eyes shifted towards him, then to the open bare yard in front of her. She didn't want him to see the fear in her eyes. People didn't choose their birthdays, but mention of that day made her blood run cold.

"What about your parents?"

"I'll call them later. They won't be happy, but they'll understand." She hoped they'd understand. Her father was a tad overprotective, but she didn't blame him under the circumstances.

"If you need me, please call. I'm always here for you."

"I know and I will." She clicked the phone off. Her and Jay's relationship had changed from booty call to him moving in with her. His male protective instinct came rushing forward. She imagined him in her bed, snuggled half beneath the fluffy comforter. Sage's boyfriend also moved in. Her best friend and surrogate sister. They had made her life, after the hospital and onslaught of memories, bearable. More than that. She loved them, and Jay.

Tommy wore only sweats that hung below his belly button. The morning sun caught the ripples of his defined chest and arm muscles. For a split second, she forgot his hair-raising birth date. He cupped his hands and blew into them. "Coffee is on. Everything OK?"

How many men would ask her that question in the matter of a couple minutes? She smiled her best fake smile and tilted her head. She needed to play it cool. "Yeah, it's cold out here. Last one in has to make breakfast." She jumped from her seat and bolted to the door, pushing him out of the way as she slid inside before him.

Snoops

Happy to get stuck with making breakfast, he made two southwestern style omelets. Cooking for her was a pleasure, something he hoped he'd be doing for a while. Although he wasn't going to stop her if she decided to go home.

Eilida handed him her key. "It's all yours. I'm staying here, and then have a class this afternoon."

He leaned in and kissed her supple lips, long and slow, wanting to make it last. "I'll see you tonight," he whispered in her ear as he brushed his lips against her cheek.

She smiled as he walked out the door and heard the unmistakable sound of the deadbolt. She didn't take chances and he adored that about her. It also made it difficult to get to know her. The mysterious air she held is probably what attracted him most.

Once inside his truck, he called *her*. If she was in New Mexico it would be seven a.m. and most likely she was still asleep with her silly eye mask on. If she was in North Carolina, she was awake, sucking down green tea. The phone rang five times and went to voice mail. He left a message.

"Where the fuck are you and why the fuck are you breaking into Eilida's apartment? I know it was you!" Yelling into the phone took away a bit of the aggression building inside him from her callous act, but not enough.

At Eilida's apartment he let himself inside. Warm sensations rushed through his body as he reminisced about their passionate moments on her couch and floor. Shaking away the memories, he looked for anything that said *she was here*. Everything looked as it had two nights ago. Eilida was a neat and orderly person.

In the kitchen, she had a few grocery bags hung on a peg. He grabbed a couple and filled them with some of Eilida's clothes. Her wardrobe was mostly jeans and T-shirts or simple blouses and hoodies. For an attractive woman she didn't flaunt it, giving her a natural beauty. Most women loaded their faces with makeup and spent hours trying to make themselves look good, but all they accomplished was making themselves look fake.

Placing the bags of clothes by the door, he crept into her bathroom and studied the window for evidence. Not a strand of blond hair, or any hair, was stuck to the window. No threads from clothing hung loose. Kneeling onto the floor, he searched for any other evidence. He scanned the wall. Nothing, absolutely nothing.

He tossed her clothes into his truck then walked around to her bathroom window. A set of small, barely visible footprints were in the dirt beneath the window. The person had tried to cover them over with dirt but the toe was still visible and appeared to be pointed toward the window, confirming someone had climbed out of it. He clicked a couple pictures, then left. *Damn her!* he thought.

She wasn't about to go back to her apartment but if he wanted to, more power to him. It gave her time to investigate him, and spending a few days with a hot guy who was born on the worst day in history wasn't as scary as a murderer breaking into her house. Maybe she was overreacting, but it wasn't happening as long as James Swan was on the loose.

Eilida didn't know what she was searching for, or even have a clear reason why she was searching. He'd never given her any reason not to trust him, but something ate away at her gut even before discovering his birthday. Inside, she hoped it was nothing, because he was quickly growing on her and, eerie feeling or not, she felt comfortable in his presence.

She milled through his townhouse and found nothing odd for a bachelor. He had a couple pornos shoved to the back of his entertainment center, but what man didn't? His computer was password protected but so was hers and most people. He had a pull-down attic and she wasn't even going up there.

When she wanted something hidden, she didn't always hide it in plain sight. She laid on the floor in the empty room and stared at the ceiling. It was a normal flat ceiling with a fan and a vent. The vent was closed, but that made sense since he didn't use the room. Nothing unusual.

Defeated, she wandered downstairs and opened her research folder, then spied his printer. She thought back to the picture of him and his parents, then opened and clicked on her computer. Finding the printer, she installed it and printed out the picture.

Then she flipped through and eyeballed the articles she'd found. Evan O'Conner was sent to Windy Oaks Mental Facility at age ten, after his entire family was slaughtered except him and Emily. Emily Turnwell, her neighbor. The bloody kitchen and two young boys with slit throats rushed through her mind, freezing on the puddles of blood beneath them and little Erica sobbing in the corner. She'd been that little girl so many years ago. The thought made her body convulse. It sickened her, yet she was compelled to understand what kind of monster could do that and why. Was he born sick in the head or did life make him that way? Everything she read pointed at his parents being abusive. *Did that drive a ten-year-old boy over the edge?*

She found what she was looking for — the lead officer in the monster's murder. Eilida jotted the number down and wrote Windy Oaks beside it, along with Evan O'Conner's childhood home address. To be an investigative reporter, she had to deal with her fears, *suck it up and be tough.*

She picked up her phone, sucked down the fear climbing through her gut and dialed the Salvation Cove police department.

The phone rang twice then a woman answered, "Salvation Cove Sheriff. What can I do ya for?"

"Officer Salyard, please?"

Demons of Ghosts Past

Tommy's phone rang and he picked it up without checking to see who was calling first. "Hello."

"Can you meet me?" she asked, her voice even.

"So you are here. What the hell?!" His fury returned.

"Yes, but you need to hear me out and not over the phone," she demanded.

The day they met entered his mind. She'd used the same tone in her voice, telling him a tale that proved to be true. She spun him into her web and now he was trapped.

He let out a deep breath. "Where?"

"At my motel room."

"Text me the address." He ended the call and raked his hand through his hair. Within seconds an address and room number shot across his screen. He whipped his SUV into the left lane and made a U-turn at the light. Pressing his foot on the gas pedal, he sped through town.

She wasn't staying at a motel but a plush hotel. He expected nothing less from her. He pushed his foot harder on the gas pedal as he sailed through the yellow light. Dodging the annoying drivers on the road, he maneuvered his SUV into the parking lot and followed the guest parking signs. He sure as hell wasn't turning his keys over to the valet.

Taking a deep breath, he calmed his growing anger and beeped the alarm on his vehicle, stuffing the keys into his pocket. A cold breeze against his back, he sauntered toward the entrance.

"How are you today, sir?" asked the doorman as he entered.

Not attempting to paint a smile on his face, he ignored him and walked straight to the elevator then pushed the up button. Glass chandeliers hung from the ceilings and plush carpet padded the floor beneath his steps. Large pots filled with colorful plants were stuck in every corner. It gave the illusion it was spring and warm, not fall and chilly.

When the doors swished open, a family of four with luggage exited. The youngest, a boy, rolled a Ninja Turtle suitcase. His coily red hair stuck out at various angles and his brown eyes set inside his round face stared at Tommy. The anger inside him melted at the sight and he gave the boy a smile and a wink. The little boy returned the smile with a dimpled one of his own, then he lifted his hand and waved as he walked past Tommy.

He slipped inside the elevator, rode to the fifth floor, and followed the jade-colored carpets. All he could think about was the millions of germs spawning in the carpet beneath his feet. When he reached room 512 he lifted his hand to knock, but she opened the door before he did so.

Her blond hair uplifted on her head and a form-fitting nightgown snuggled against her body. He had to admit she kept her age well and didn't look a day over twenty-five. She took a few steps backward and he closed the door behind him.

"What the hell are you doing?" he demanded, stepping towards her.

Calm and cool, she held her stance and responded, "Giving you a shove in the right direction."

He took another step towards her and she turned on her heels, strolling towards the window. She picked up a steaming cup, then turned facing him and took a sip. Calm and calculating; he loved and hated that about her. On one hand, he wished he had that kind of control over his own emotions; on the other hand, it was a trait genetically passed to Evan.

He leaned his tall frame against the wall. "I had everything under control." *More than you know.*

"Is that what you call it?"

"Yeah, that's what I call it," he seethed.

"I took advantage of a situation. A dead girl, a crazy, guilty boyfriend who *disappeared*." She set her tea down and padded towards Tommy, brushing her hand against his smooth-shaven chin. "Where is she now, Dil?"

His first thought was *she did it.* She killed the girl and framed the boyfriend, but Tommy had questioned him, grilled him until he heard the entire story. He narrowed his eyes. "At my townhouse... Did you kill that girl?" *Killing wasn't her style, but he wouldn't put anything past her. She was a survivor.*

"That's what you think? I must be as psycho as Evan? Damnit you know me better than that!" Her eyes blazed, the green one almost black and the amber eye shooting fire. *He'd pushed her Evan button.*

"No, Scar, I don't think you killed her. You took advantage of a situation and frightened a young lady who, like yourself, has been through hell." He eased toward the bed and sat on the edge.

She scooted onto the bed beside him and smoothed his hair. "You're the son I wish I'd had. You know? You're strong and smart and have you looked in the mirror lately? You're a complete stud." She sighed. "There's a bond between you and Eilida like the bond between us. We're all victims of the same craziness. Have you asked her about her nightmares?"

Tommy stared at the floor and winced, but didn't respond.

"Have you done anything besides fuck her?"

He cocked his head toward her with a scowl on his face. "I'm getting there. She's fragile and has a tough exterior."

"She's also smart. Smart enough to recall details a two-year-old should never remember."

They sat silent for a minute. It was Eilida's memories that cracked the case and led police to Evan, and connected his crimes and the title *The Hurricane Killer*. It infuriated him that she was right, he just didn't understand why she was so desperate for him and Eilida to crack the case. And, if Eilida knew his part, she'd never speak with him again.

The guilt lay on his heart heavy as the densest black hole.

"And don't give me a guilt trip about this. I know what you did to that kid." She hadn't witnessed anything, as she'd only just arrived, but she knew him. And it didn't hurt that he thought she witnessed his indiscretion.

Tommy whipped his head towards her. "Are you following me?!" He jumped off the bed. "And he was guilty as hell. The little bastard killed her because she wouldn't allow him to drug and ass-fuck her!"

She half-smiled. "Calm down, big boy. He was a creepy kid. Your actions are justified as far as I'm concerned."

Whenever Tommy needed an escape, he sought her. His grandfather was always grumpy and grandma waited on him like a slave. Grandpa was impossible to please; the lawn is too high, it's too low, the car isn't clean enough, wax it again. Nothing he did was ever right and when he disappeared for a time they never went looking. He figured they enjoyed life better when he wasn't there. Living with Evan was far easier and enjoyable than the Gramps.

As a teen, he ran to Scarlett's. After a few months, he discovered the house wasn't hers. She was simply a house sitter and it was time for her to move on. They stayed in contact through email and text. She'd visit him from time to time. His own mother killed when he was a mere fifteen, she took on the roll and he loved her even when she infuriated him.

Tommy left Scarlett's hotel room and made a stop at the small locker he rented. He pulled out a bag labeled "3" and stuffed the object underneath the back seat of his Lexus.

Eilida called the Salvation Cove police department only to find out the lead investigator in Evan O'Conner's case had quit and was now employed as a detective in Horn City. She gave him a call and he agreed to meet with her at Wilson's Café.

Horn City was only a two-hour drive and at this hour traffic was light. When she entered the café, her eyes scanned the tables and saw a gentleman with dirty blond hair stand up and wave her towards him. When she approached, she realized he had a few gray hairs and small webs creasing from the corners of his brown eyes.

"Ms. Riley, nice to meet you," he said, grasping her hand and shaking.

"Mr. Salyard. Thank you for taking the time." She took a seat on the checkered cloth bench across from him, matching red and white checkered curtains hung in the windows, drawn back with red ties.

He grimaced. "You're a star."

She felt her cheeks flush with heat. "I'm not here because of any of that. Think of me as a student."

He widened his eyes and nodded. The décor in the place was light and the cloth bench was comfy beneath her butt. She cleared her throat. "Do you mind if I record this? It makes it easier when I'm typing."

"Not at all."

"You were the lead investigator in The Hurricane Killer, Evan O'Conner's death. Were you also the first to arrive on the scene?" Saying the monster's name made her cringe.

The waitress walked up, bringing her a glass of water, setting a sandwich in front of him and handing her a menu. "Thank you," Eilida responded. She was stuffed from her snack of peanut butter-filled pretzels on the ride over and had no intention of eating again, even though the scents of cooked meat and bacon were mouth-watering.

"At the time, I was a small-town deputy and was the closest when the call came in, so I responded and was the first to arrive." He unfolded his sandwich and squeezed mayo and mustard onto it.

"Can you describe the scene?"

"It wasn't pretty, but it was clean. Whoever murdered him thought long and hard about it." He paused. "It was premeditated." He took a bite of his sandwich.

This wasn't exactly news. She wanted something not in the papers. "What do you mean by clean?"

He swallowed. "There was plenty of blood, all the vics… Evan O'Conner's, but no trace of who did it."

No need for names, the monster works for me, she thought.

"No murder weapon, no DNA. Nothing. There's speculation it was a one of his victims but that's not what I saw." He took another bite of his sandwich and swallowed after only a couple chews. "My guess is a contract killing, but with no evidence the trail went cold." His jaw slacked.

She found that interesting the fact that his speculation was never printed. She leaned in, turned off her recorder and lifted her eyebrows. "I need an A paper. Is there anything you can tell me about the scene that wasn't printed in the papers?"

His left eyelid twitched as he pulled a cell phone from his pocket, pushed the screen a few times and said, "This." He held it in front of her. It was a picture of a ring.

She reached out her hand. "Can I?" she asked.

He nodded.

She studied the picture. It looked identical to the zircon ring she'd given to Sage that went missing at the astrology convention. It wasn't custom made or special in any way, but what are the odds that the killer had the same ring? *Or was it the monster's ring?*

Eilida handed him back the phone. "Is there any significance to the ring?"

He shrugged. "We researched it, seems it has astrological significance. Evan O'Conner was into that stuff, so I'm guessing it was his. At first, I thought maybe," he curled his lips downward, "it was a calling card. Some kind of vigilante, but there haven't been any similar crimes reported nationwide. If it has significance, we never figured it out."

There was a small hole in the cloth bench and her nervous finger found it, drilling into the cushion. Swishing her lips back and forth she weighed the informational value of the ring. "I had a ring just like that. When I learned it was an Attractor, I gave it to my friend. Nothing bad ever happens in her life, but I've always suffered nightmares." Her finger dug deeper into the hole.

"An Attractor, huh?" He pulled at his chin. "Maybe it wasn't a calling card, but communication from his killer. Evan, The Hurricane Killer, spent a lifetime attracting negative energy. He's harmed so many people, destroyed so many families. That ring may be a message."

She hadn't thought of it that way. Stripping her hand from the hole she'd made worse with her finger, she placed it on her lap. The answer was in the astrology. The notes she'd gathered were useful, but the answers lay in the charts. *Did the monster have charts?* Speculation said he did. Even though they were never found, enough astrology-related stuff was found in his home.

The Cycle of Abuse

The Next Day

The sun high in the sky and the fall air chilly, Burkhalder walked into the funeral home. The Mora girl lay peacefully sleeping on her silken bed. An older couple, seated, holding hands, the woman dabbing a tissue at her eyes, sat in the front row. She assumed they were Chelsea's guardians.

She walked towards the casket. The young woman lay peaceful. Her oval face solemn. Burkhalder's heart sank. The Moras were not good people and she could only imagine the abuse the young girl survived as a child. At three and a half, she wasn't old enough to voice it herself, but investigations arose after the deaths of her family.

Burkhalder never shed a tear for the Moras, only their innocent son who Evan also murdered. The violent slayings of her family and the abuse she suffered as a child, it wasn't a surprise she'd "fallen in love" with a violent man.

James Swan was still at large. The police were talking with family, friends, professors, and other students but he'd evaded everyone. Taking a seat in the back row, she observed the crowd, waiting for one man whom she believed would be there.

As everyone took their seats, she scanned the room. After several sweeps, she found him. The snug fit of his sleeves over his triceps gave hints to his well-defined frame. She kept one eye on him throughout the ceremony.

She left the sanctuary and stood inside the front room as the ceremony was finishing. When everyone filed out, she watched him pay his condolences and stroll past her. Almost every bit as tall as him she strode beside him. "Tyrus Reed."

He cocked his head and gave her a questioning look. "Do I know you?"

"No, but I know a little about you and why you're here. Do you have a minute?"

He nodded as if he knew the day would come. "Walk with me, Ms. Burkhalder."

Burkhalder wrapped her coat around her middle to keep her body warm against the nippy air. Now that was a surprise. *How did he know her?*

Noting the shocked expression on her face, he continued, "You're the woman who pieced together the crimes of *The Hurricane Killer* and you think I know something because I escaped."

He was reading her mind. Not only did she think he knew something, but maybe thought he was involved with Evan's murder.

They reached his car, a black BMW — he was a man of taste. She sucked in a breath, impressed with the smooth nature of the young man. "Yes, on all accounts."

He walked around to the passenger door and opened it. "Ride with me and I'll fill you in."

She nodded and sank into the smooth, leather seat. He closed the door and went around to the driver's side. As he maneuvered the car into the line of traffic, something caught her eye. A tall man with a blond ponytail, but she couldn't be sure. Straining her neck, she watched him bob in and out of the crowd. Instead of walking with the crowd, he walked against it.

"Something catch your eye?" he asked, cocking his head towards her.

"Yeah, can you pull over for a minute?"

"As slow as traffic is moving I'd be happy to," he said with a dimpled smile.

"Thanks." She kept her eye on the other man as he entered the church carrying something. Tyrus stopped the car and she glanced his direction. "I'll be right back."

Running around the crowd, she made it to the church and slowed her pace as she entered. Craning her neck, she scanned the inside of the church, but she didn't see him anywhere. She proceeded inside the sanctuary.

With caution, she approached the casket. A brown bear lay beside Chelsea Mora's chest. *A souvenir?* Serial killers often take souvenirs. Evan took them from the girls and the blond man, whoever he was, had returned *Chelsea's bear.* She remembered a conversation with Eilida about her monkey *Sandy* appearing out of nowhere on the table beside Eilida's hospital bed. In delirium, then in a coma for a week Eilida didn't know how it got there.

A touch on her shoulder made Burkhalder jump. Her heart beating fast, she looked behind her.

Savior Evan

The kind blue eyes of the pastor looked at her. "I didn't mean to startle you."

Catching her breath, she scanned the room. They were alone but she noted a door to her left. "Where does that lead?"

Furrowing his brow, he answered, "To the offices."

"Is there a back door?"

"Yes, it leads to the staff parking."

She hated to do it at the poor girl's funeral but the cops needed to be called, the bear may contain important DNA evidence.

"Call the police. That bear," she pointed to the stuffed animal beside the dead young woman, "is evidence. I'll explain more later." She pushed the heavy wood door open and raced down the hall. Sure enough, at the end of the hall was a glass door. She pushed through into the parking lot. A red truck sped off but she wasn't close enough to make out the license plate. Although she knew the make and model, a black Lexus SUV.

Back inside the church, she found the confused pastor and began explaining the story, starting with Chelsea Mora. Tyrus walked into the church. He strolled towards her with a smile. It disappeared as he approached them.

"What happened?" he asked, concern in his voice.

She pointed towards the casket. His eyes glanced downward to the dead woman, then towards Burkhalder, his eyes widened. *Recognition?* Yes, he remembered far more than he told the police. His behavior suggested he was going to tell her everything anyways. It would just have to wait.

The police walked through the door. "Can you wait?" she asked Tyrus. He nodded.

She approached the officers and once again explained the situation. As she talked with them she thought back to Emily Turnwell. *Was a souvenir left at her funeral?* She didn't think so because she would have remembered and it wouldn't make sense. Evan was carted off the night he slaughtered his family. He wouldn't have had the chance to keep a souvenir. But what about the day he killed Emily? *Did he take a toy of her daughter Erica's?* If so, it wasn't found at Evan's death scene only hours later. A child's toy wouldn't have stuck out as odd since the Turnwells had three children. Then it dawned on her, it wasn't what was left but what was taken.

The police bagged the bear for evidence and swabbed the casket and door for finger prints. What a horrible day and how sad this happened during the young woman's funeral, as if her life hadn't been filled with enough violence and sadness. Tears formed in the corners of her eyes. And the young woman's family looked at her with disdain and fear. Their mouths in straight lines and eyes widened.

She approached Chelsea's guardians. "I'm truly sorry for your loss and this mess."

The man held his wife and smoothed her hair. "At her funeral. Who would do this? I thought the monster was dead?"

"He is. I can assure you."

"Then who and why?" he growled.

She understood, but had no answer. "I don't know. I hope the police can answer that question after forensics test the bear."

He shook his head.

Without further response she left the church. Tyrus waited outside for her.

"Thank you for waiting. Where were we?"

He smiled. "Going for a drive. Shall we?"

He pulled out of the church parking lot. She liked the young man already. He was a gentleman.

Once they exited the parking lot and headed down the road, he started his story. "The day the Moras took me, I didn't see their faces. As I said, they got me from behind and shot something into my neck that put me to sleep. I woke up in a dark room without any recollection of how I got there. My mind was foggy but I heard voices. When the door opened, a man came in. The room was dark and I acted like I was asleep. He left a plate of food in the room and a glass of water. Sometime later he returned. He took me down the hall to a restroom. I hadn't ate their food or drank their water but my bladder was full from fear pumping through my veins. I didn't care that he watched. I just didn't want to pee my pants."

Burkhalder envisioned the young boy, filled with fear. Her heart heavy for him.

"He took me back to the room. I kept my mouth closed and observed my surroundings. We walked by a little girl's room and she looked at me with wide eyes. The bear clutched to her chest. The man, Mr. Mora I assume, closed the door and forced a needle into my arm. The next time I awoke a different man came into my room. I couldn't see his face but his form was much thicker than the other man. Once he laid eyes on me he closed and locked the door. It locked from the outside. After that there was a lot of commotion and dense footsteps halted at the room I was locked in. The knob twisted and the thick man entered, demanding to know where I lived. I was scared and did pee myself a little that time, then the man softened and told me he was taking me out of there. I scurried towards him and followed his directions."

"Evan. It was Evan O'Conner," shot out of Burkhalder's mouth.

He nodded. "Only he told me his name was Nyle. He rescued me and took me home. It wasn't until I was much older that I realized who he was. He saved my life and even though he was scary I couldn't see him the way the papers painted. So I never came forward."

"Instead you earned a black belt and became a defense attorney." The creases in her forehead furrowed. His calm speech and facial expressions said he was being honest with her, but everything else said guilty.

He nodded. "Nobody was ever kidnapping me again, although, I've never used my skills other than competition and teaching. Karate teaches discipline. And yes, I defend those accused of crimes. They aren't all guilty, and as you are probably thinking, it was my experience that set me on the path. The Moras were guilty but Mr. O'Conner, guilty or not, protected me from them. There's a good side in everyone."

"Not Evan. He most likely considered killing you before he decided to rescue you. But you didn't fit his type and followed his directions. Don't think if you'd spoken up while he was alive that he wouldn't have murdered you and your family."

He cracked a half smile. "Agreed. And what I've told you stays with us," his face growing solemn, "I'm a grown man and able to protect myself, but after what I saw today he has an accomplice who's not finished."

The Day of Death

Eilida took notes mindlessly. She couldn't focus on what her teacher was saying. When she looked at her notebook scribbles a large, jagged blade filled the paper. She ripped it from her notebook and wadded it. Then her bag vibrated. She pulled out her phone – Patrice. ¬ She had to get this. Scrunching the paper into a tiny ball and grasping her phone, she left her seat and strolled towards the door, dropping the paper in the wastebasket.

"Hello, Patrice. Thank you for returning my call," she said, once in the hallway and outside of class.

"Eilida, nice to hear from you. How have you been?" Her effervescent voice bubbled in Eilida's ears and brought a smile to her face.

"I'm doing well. But…" she paused, feeling as though she was using her.

"I'm here to help. Do you need some astrological advice?" She could almost see her eyebrows furrow on her face into a V.

"I do. Um… A friend of mine. It's more complicated than that. I met this guy at the convention and we coincidentally met here. He attends the same college, but it gets weirder."

"Go on," she gently nudged.

Eilida spilled the horrid story, sparing only the goriest details as she paced the hallway outside the lecture hall. Then included how *her friend* was born the day of the hurricane, in the same town.

"Oh, so you're wanting a natal chart for this Dillon who goes by Tommy."

"Yes, please. I'd be happy to pay, please send me a bill ¬."

Patrice cut her off midsentence. "For you, I'll do it free of charge. After that story, I'm curious. I remember reading about it in the papers and I'll do whatever I can to help."

Eilida sank onto a bench in the hallway, relief filling her up. "Thank you!" Tommy's chart was a start until she went through everything, gathering enough info about the monster to have his completed. There was something about Tommy that nagged at her. Born on the day her family was slaughtered was too much of a coincidence. It didn't make him guilty of a crime, but was more a call to action.

"My pleasure. Email me his birthdate, time, and place. I assume he's living where you are now. I'll get it done today and we can go over the results."

"Thank you so much!"

"You're welcome."

Eilida opened the bulky door and slipped back to her seat, hoping her absence went unnoticed. She pulled Patrice's card out of her wallet and emailed her Tommy's info.

Tommy snatched his truck keys from the counter and headed to the gym to blow off his pent up anger. He adjusted the weight on the bar and laid on the bench. Without a spotter, he began to lift the weight. One of the employees ran towards him.

"You need a spotter, safety first." The young man urged. Tommy continued lifting.

He paused for a second. "I guess you're it."

The young man took one look at the amount of weight on the bar and nodded. "OK, hold on."

Tommy continued. He knew the risks but didn't care. The one thing he

and Evan had in common was they were
both born under the Cancer sign. Evan
didn't know that. There was a lot Evan
didn't know about Tommy, like his real
name was Dillon. He used the name
Tommy to play it safe and she made him
a fake ID to match. Over time, the name
grew to fit him and rarely anymore did he
use the name Dillon. Tommy hadn't ever
been one to believe in silly stuff like
astrology but after what happened he
became a believer of sorts, and Cancers
weren't always rational.

The young employee came back
to Tommy with one of their trainers. A
large man with bulging muscles. Tommy
smiled, the boy was scrawny and would
have been a waste as a spotter.

The trainer didn't bother to make
small talk. That was good. Tommy was in
no mood to listen or talk. He finished up
his set, thanked him, and moved to
squats. The trainer continued spotting
him and Tommy's mind worked through
his thoughts.

Evan's wandering eyes. He
looked at him from the first moment
with lust. Tommy felt it and, the longer
he knew him, the more creeped out it
made him feel. He'd noticed the tent in
Evan's pants when he was near him and
it was all he could do to swallow his own

vomit. When he touched him, his skin crawled with thousands of tiny bugs. When he pretended to want him so he could lunge the syringe into his neck and end his life, he had to remind himself of the reason he was doing it.

Two years living with him, he loathed him. Yet, he admired him. They had many of the same interests in cooking and music. Evan wasn't all bad. There was a side to him that was gentle and even timid. Inside, he was a scared boy who was traumatized beyond the point of being helped. His fucked up genetics made sure of that.

He finished his workout and showered. With a towel around his waist, he messaged Eilida. Evan was her worst nightmare. Since meeting her, he'd been glad that a force had intervened and kept her alive. If Evan hadn't died, she was next on his list. He was killing them in the order he had slaughtered their families. Evan was methodical in his ways and controlled. He didn't make silly decisions, except when it came to Tommy. He cringed at the memory, as he was the only person Evan allowed close enough to him, making Tommy numero uno in the murder plan.

Setting his phone on the bench, he dressed and brushed his hair. He glanced at his phone several times before picking it back up. Nothing. Looking at the time, he realized it was getting late, so he stopped at the store. He hadn't cooked her dinner the night of the break in so tonight he would.

House Guest

Unlocking her phone, she noticed Tommy had left a message. He was going to the store and planned on cooking her dinner. The blinking email light begged her attention. Touching the email icon, a message from Patrice popped up. Almost unable to contain her excitement, she opened it. A natal chart was attached at the bottom and the message read: *Here is the chart, call me after you've read it and we'll talk about it.*

Her insides rolled as she opened the document. The last thing she wanted was bad news, mostly because she wanted to trust him. She eyeballed the chart but had trouble interpreting all the lines, then began reading...

Cautious, prudent, and rather self-contained, you are a person who approaches life realistically and who is not inclined to take foolish chances or get carried away by the overly optimistic or idealistic schemes of starry-eyed dreamers. In fact, you frequently have a jaundiced view of such things. You are rather worldly-wise from a fairly young age, even something of a cynic. Often, the world doesn't seem like a safe, friendly place to you, and you tend to approach life in a guarded, conservative manner. You are generally calculating and careful, and are rarely spontaneous, fluid, open, and childlike.

So far that's him. She continued reading until she got to the end.

Finishing up her notes from class, she closed her notebook and slid it inside her denim bag, then waved to Mrs. Rixley and headed to Tommy's. She'd stayed there since her place was broken into. He hadn't complained and she didn't plan on returning home until James Swan was found and hauled off to jail.

His SUV was absent when she pulled in his driveway and she sighed with relief as she'd have the privacy to call Patrice. The excitement inside her fizzed over as she picked up her phone. A part of her still felt bad that she was getting free help, yet, the other part of her was grateful and anxious to learn whatever she could.

"Hello," bubbled Patrice's voice.

"It's Eilida. I just read his chart."

Patrice let out a breath. "First I have to tell you we only read a chart to the person it belongs, but in your case, I sense your concern. This must stay between us." Her bubbly voice grew solemn. "Where do we start? What I sent you is the information my astrological software generates. There's a lot more to Tommy than what it says, since those reports don't cover the subtle parts that only a trained astrologer can detect. What is your overall impression of him? Is there something about him that worries you? Or do you feel good about him?"

Eilida tensed further, wondering what Patrice had found that made her ask such a thing. "I'm not sure. There's something about him that bothers me, but I can't put my finger on it. I get a good feeling from him, yet he seems deceptive. If that makes any sense."

"Completely," Patrice responded. "Remember that anything in a person's chart can go either way. A person always has free will and can use the energy as he or she wants. But there are some aspects that can be difficult to manage. The energy can be overwhelming and what their life has been like, whether they've had positive or negative experiences to program their mind, will drive their reaction."

"So just because someone has bad aspects doesn't mean they'll be a bad person, but they could be if they've had bad experiences?" Eilida asked.

"Exactly. For one thing, he was born under a solar eclipse. Crazy stuff happens, disasters of all types, but we should always look at things in the positive. He's a planner, loves the finer aesthetics in life. He isn't afraid to take a chance and will protect what he believes in."

Eilida thought back to the horrible night of Hurricane Chloe. It had been a solar eclipse? That was new to her. She guessed it just hadn't been important until now. She also thought about his new Lexus and chuckled inside as Patrice said 'finer aesthetics'.

Eilida kept her mouth closed as Patrice continued.

"That Capricorn ascendant will make him serious, organized, and willing to take the lead or responsibility. He's not frivolous or flighty. Saturn in the first house will strengthen that. Saturn is in a condition known as interception. That happens when a sign, in this case Aquarius, is contained entirely within a house. That means the energy has no way of getting out, it's trapped. It can build up, needing expression that's difficult to find. Saturn is also part of a pattern I call a course adjustment loop. It looks like a triangle that has a red, blue and green side. This will help Saturn express itself, mainly with regard to taking responsibility."

That struck a chord with Eilida. He'd rescued her the night they bumped into each other at *Flashers*. She made a bad decision to cut through the woods and freaked when she saw the teens. Their wide eyes and frozen stances told her they were just as surprised as she was. But Tommy acted as if it was up to him to save her. And he was here now, allowing her to stay in his home, saving her from unknown danger. She shoved the thought to a corner of her mind and continued focusing on Patrice's words.

Her mind deep in thought, processing everything Patrice told her, she thanked her and hung up the phone. Everything she said made sense as far as Eilida knew him. Even the love factor. She felt an unnatural attraction to him, enough she was ready to go to bed with him even though she had a boyfriend. One that had been there for her when she needed him. The vibes she got from Tommy were mixed. She felt the attraction, yet at the same time, felt his hesitation.

She focused for a minute on a single part of his chart. Patrice had said, *'There's another caution flag on his chart with Neptune, the planet of deception, conjunct his ascendant. This implies that people will not see him as he really is.'* What is he hiding?

113

Tommy stood outside the front door of his townhouse, grocery bags draped over his left arm. The keys jingling in his right hand. He was poised to unlock the door when he heard Eilida's voice. *Who is she talking to?* he asked himself. There was no other car in his driveway, or even parked along the street outside his home.

Curious, he tilted his head, facing an ear to the door, attempting to eavesdrop on the conversation. He heard muffled garble and something that sounded like *childhood pain* and the word *him*. Yes, he clearly heard the word him but who is *him*?

Tommy shuddered at the thought of his own childhood pain, not all of it Evan's fault but the part that inhaled and exhaled inside his head was Evan's fault entirely. The reason he couldn't let it go.

Taking a deep breath and flushing the memory down the virtual toilet in his head, he unlocked the door and went straight to the kitchen. Dropping the grocery bags on the island counter top he took out the groceries, organizing them as he went.

Eilida strolled into the kitchen. She didn't walk up to him, instead pulled out a chair, her eyes not leaving Tommy, and planted herself on it. She twisted a lock of hair. Her behavior suggested something wasn't right in her world and Tommy hoped it had nothing to do with him.

Since the townhouse was empty except for her, he surmised she'd been on the phone. *Did she know something about him?* Breaking the silence, anticipating her conversation had nothing to do with him he asked, "Something wrong?"

Her chest heaved. "Not really. I have a lot of work to do for a final project in my investigative journalism class. You're studying criminal justice, maybe you can help me?" Eilida didn't know how much he knew about the significance of his birthday and thought she'd bring him in. It was also a test to study his reaction.

Tommy pulled out a knife as he arranged vegetables on a large wooden cutting board. "Sure, we can work on it after dinner."

Reliving the Past

Burkhalder thought of the young, tall, blond man and scanned through all her notes. Nobody ever mentioned him, or Evan ever having a friend or companion. *Where did he come from?* Without a doubt she pegged him as Evan's murderer since he was last person anyone saw Evan alive with and *when did he hook up with him, after killing the Turnwells?*

She hurried outside to Frank detailing the interior of his truck. Frank lifted his head when he saw the flash of Alice Burkhalder, his girlfriend and business partner, rush towards his truck.

"What's gotcha?" he asked, knowing her too well.

"The blond. He was at the funeral."

He set the rag down and stepped outside his truck. "Are we talking Evan O'Conner?"

She folded her arms and leaned against his truck. Her head cocked towards Frank. "Yes, he's the key, but how do we find him?"

"You mean Evan's murderer. I thought you didn't want to pursue this?" He leaned beside her against his newly washed/waxed and sparkling truck.

"I didn't until now. The Mora girl, going to her funeral and seeing her brought the twenty years of chasing Evan back. I can't walk away just because someone got to him before I did." He'd been away on business and missed it, although she'd kept him filled in during their daily phone calls.

A chilly breeze made her shiver, as she hadn't put on a jacket before rushing outside. He wrapped his arm around her.

"That's it," he chuckled. "Someone else, not you. Honey, I understand better than anyone how that must eat you up inside. Remember we met the night he murdered the Moras, I wanted to nail that SOB too. Drag out the files and I'll meet you inside."

She smiled. "They're already out. I guess you haven't been inside the office since you returned."

His eyes twinkled. "I should have known." He patted her ass as she walked past him and rushed to get out of the cold.

She stopped and turned towards him for a second. "Someone dropped a brown teddy bear into Chelsea's coffin. It came back clean, no prints, no DNA. What's your take?"

He rubbed his chin and twisted his lips. "An accomplice, the young man I saw him with, or maybe we have a new villain, Dexter type, who kills bad guys and returns trophies to victims."

She pursed her lips. "We need to find that young man," she said, then rushed towards the house and heat.

A few minutes later, he sauntered into the office. Burkhalder on the floor with every file laid out before her. The date May, 8 2014, written on the large whiteboard and names drawn from it.

"You've been busy. But we need to go back. Who do we know that had any connection to Evan?"

She leaned back and laid her head against the floor. "The lawyer, Mr. Fritz. He knew a heck of a lot more than he ever let on—"

Frank interrupted her, "What about the lady we met at his gate? A housekeeper. She'd know everything and maybe now that he's gone she'd be willing to talk."

A quizzical smile graced Burkhalder's face. "I'd forgotten about her." Then another thought manifested in her head. "Scarlett!" She lifted herself upwards, her eyes scanning the folders. She found the one she wanted and opened it up. "Here," she pointed.

Frank leaned down and gripped the other end of the folder, reading it along with her. Years ago she'd interviewed a young woman, Misty, who lived next door to Evan before he inherited his fortune and specifically mentioned an anomaly in his eyes. Around his pupils he had two different colored rings.

He took a seat on one of the spinning comfy computer chairs, letting go of his grasp on the folder. "A search we need to renew. At the least to identify her as his biological mother."

A wide smile spread across Burkhalder's face. "And Scarlett has blond hair. The blond man you saw with Evan. How old would you say he was?"

He tugged at his chin. "I never got a clear view of his face, but didn't look older than twenty-something."

Burkhalder's eyes wide. "It's a long shot, but if she had Evan at a young age then this other when she was older. This kid could be hers too."

While Tommy cooked dinner, Eilida laid out all her notes and copies of information she gained from the college library and her interview. Chills scuttled over her body and her eye involuntarily twitched as she studied the info. The memories of that day would never leave her, but she couldn't think Tommy inherently evil because he was born during hurricane Chloe while she was hiding from the evil man.

It was a fluke, but bothered her, tugging at her guts as her mind correlated the events of that day while looking at the newspaper article of his parents. His mother holding a tiny Tommy in her arms. She debated on whether she'd show him that picture. *Did he know?*

The scent of garlic infused the air and her stomach grumbled in hunger. She padded into the kitchen and gasped. He'd turned the lights down so a gentle glow illuminated the room. A candle burned on the center of the kitchen table. Two plates with garlic chicken on fettuccini covered with a white sauce and seasoned vegetables sat on opposite sides of the table along with silverware laid on gold fabric napkins. The candlelight bounced against the bottle of red wine placed next to it.

Tommy walked towards a stunned Eilida and grasped her hand in his, guiding her to a chair. He pulled it out and after she sat he pushed it back in, then slid a gold napkin off the table and lay it on her lap. He poured red wine into her glass until it was half-full and walked around the table, taking the other seat. "You're just in time," he said, smiling as he shook out his napkin and placed it on his lap.

In awe, Eilida took in the scene in front of her. Patrice's words lingered in her head: *He may react emotionally in ways that are unrealistic. He may have poor judgment as far as who he cares for or falls in love with. Following your heart is usually a good thing, but he may not always do so in a positive way. What he wants he'll pursue... He won't always see things as they really are, at least as far as social norms are concerned.'* Was this display an example?

Choking down her own insecurities and paranoia, she returned his smile then remembered her manners. In a quiet voice, she said, "It's very beautiful. Thank you."

Sleeping With the Enemy

Eilida's eyes fluttered open and for a second she forgot she was in Tommy's bed. Her heartbeat quickened then she smelled the scent of Tommy's aftershave and remembered where she was. She turned over and glanced at Tommy, sleeping peacefully. The fluffy comforter pulled to just above his waist and his body lying on its side facing the door. In her past life, this is when she'd slip out, but under the circumstances she wasn't going anywhere. James Swan was still out there, somewhere. And to be honest with herself, she enjoyed his company and his sweet gestures, regardless of her reservations about his character.

Tommy's back moving in and out with each breath. Lying in bed next to a man she knew very little about, yet she felt safe. *What is it about him?*

She couldn't answer her own question and crawled out of bed. Tiptoeing across the floor in the dark, keeping one eye on Tommy, she lifted her robe off the hook just inside the opened bathroom door and slipped it on, wrapping it across her body and tying it to fight the chill in the air. She didn't want to wake him, as he had an early class. When she reached the stairs, she placed one foot at a time in slow motion on each step and clutched the railing. When she hit the second to bottom step it made a small creak. Reaching the bottom, she slid her hand along the wall and felt for the light switch, then flipped it on.

She padded to the kitchen, where Tommy had left the stove light on and poured herself a glass of water. Leaning her back against the counter, she sipped at the water, deep in thought. She recalled the fearful night of May 8 and Hurricane Chloe but other details while she was in the hospital were fuzzy. Her instincts told her to remember Tommy, but he had nothing to do with her accident and she ignored the creepy feeling inside her. Since she felt safe with him, pushing the creepy feeling down was easy. The conundrum was between her instincts and memories and she was leaving it at that.

Sitting cross-legged on the living room floor, she blinked back tears and frightening memories as she sorted through and catalogued the hurricanes, starting with Chloe. She'd been the little girl left behind. In 1995, he struck again. Hurricane Darlene had blown through Florida and another little girl lost her family to Evan.

In 1998, a hurricane battered the east coast, South Carolina. This scene was a little different. The house was burned down, a young boy escaped and the girl was found outside the home. She let go of the paper and it floated to the ground. These girls wouldn't be much younger than her. Figuring up the math, the first girl would be twenty-three maybe twenty-four. The next girl would be about twenty, possibly twenty-one. Suddenly she had an urge to meet them and talk with them. Grasping the paper again, she read further. Her name was *Mora*.

She mulled over the name for a couple seconds before realizing why it sounded familiar. Since the accident, her memory wasn't quite as sharp as it had been. Mora was the last name of the student killed on campus in her dorm room. But it was a semi-popular name, so she shrugged off any possible connection.

Scribbling down a few details, such as the city and last name, she ripped the paper off the tablet and pushed it to the side. She'd try calling the police departments to get info about each girl. A smile set on her face. She wasn't alone. It wasn't that she wasn't aware that he'd left behind other girls, she just hadn't considered the possibility of meeting them. As the excitement of a mini victim support group grew inside her head, an intense fear cropped up. *Did they remember? It might be better to leave them alone than bring up fearful memories.*

She continued with her notes until she came to another date that stood out. July 13, 2007, was his final Hurricane Kill. The police suspected he'd been injured but found no definitive evidence, however, after that date he didn't kill again until May 8, 2014. A roll of thunder vibrated through the clouds. Eilida's body involuntarily jumped and her heart leaped into her chest. Pulling her arms across her chest, she grabbed her shoulders and squeezed, while bringing her knees to her chest.

She used the breathing skills she learned to calm down and chanted in a barely audible whisper. *The storm can't hurt you.* She didn't know if she'd ever get over the terror storms created inside her.

Once calm, she returned to her train of thought. *Why did he wait so long?* She thought about the dates again. They were always three years apart. Her eyes shifted from one pile to the next, then picked up the picture of baby Tommy and she thought of Burkhalder. She was a Billows Hollow police officer then. All of a sudden, something she'd said to her as Eilida recovered in the hospital came to her: 'He used astrology.' Det. Salyard too.

Why wasn't that ever printed? If he believed in astrology, he'd have his natal chart and other charts for each day. Did the police find them and keep it from the public? The detective only mentioned the ring, so she assumed no charts were ever found. She read *Whobeda's Guide to Basic Astrology*. Since it was signed by the author, she didn't dog ear the corners of the pages or highlight the important parts instead she put sticky notes throughout and bought *Definitive Guide to Astrological Reports* written by the same author – Whobeda – to help her interpret and understand the various types of charts. Even so, she didn't feel she knew enough to interpret charts. Her ability was somewhere between beginner and intermediate. She still needed Patrice to help.

Rain streamed across the sliding glass door only feet from her, but she didn't notice as her mind was focused on a thought, something that would set her paper apart from everyone else's. The stars dictated his actions and, if he was a believer, he used them to determine his course of actions. *What else about him did the police keep quiet?*

Burkhalder. She'd call her. After all, she'd chased him for decades and would know details never released. Covering her mouth with one hand as she yawned, she lay the picture of Tommy and his parents down on the stack with the other hand, grabbed her water and padded towards the sliding glass window. Rivulets of water poured down the screen and she choked back her instant panic, forcing herself to face it.

"Mom, where are you?" she called to the air. "You showed me the way before, show me again." A creak caught her attention and she whipped her head towards it.

Tommy awoke when he felt the cool air rush against his back. In a couple days, he'd grown used to having Eilida beside him. He enjoyed having her around and purposely made a romantic dinner to avoid assisting her. He didn't think he'd be able to quell his distaste for

Evan, or his emotional response. That's what scared him the most. Keeping his emotions in check was difficult to do even in stealth *Tommy* mode.

This was his mission, so why was it so hard for him? It hadn't been hard to fake his mother's death. He and Scarlett planned it out meticulously. She'd called him when she spotted Evan spying on the neighbors. Scarlett, as devious as Evan, spent her years jumping from one house sitting job to the next throughout hurricane prone areas, watching and waiting for him.

His mind remembered the incident clearly. When she called him, he rushed over. She stood in front of the window, her back towards it and he swung the fire poker, stopping just before connecting with her head. Scarlett dropped and crawled to another room in the house not visible from the road. Tommy loaded a large suitcase with heavy objects to give it weight, and padded them with a down comforter so they wouldn't shift and give away what they were and packed it into the trunk of Scarlett's car. They needed Evan to believe he'd stuffed his mother inside the suitcase.

Evan bought it. The emotionally driven side of him didn't question what was in the suitcase. He thought he was doing Tommy a favor. Tommy told him what Scarlett coached him to say, that his mother was abusive, and it worked. As they coasted down the road to dump the *body*, Tommy fought the anxiety inside him. He was in a car with the man who murdered his best friend and who he'd smashed a heavy paperweight against. Although, he wasn't one hundred percent sure. From the back, he looked like the same guy, but he'd never actually seen his face. He was a scared kid and ran, bumping into Scarlett. That's how they met.

A nervous swarm of bees beat against his insides as they unloaded the *body*. A warm day, his nervous fear-induced sweat was covered by heat from the sun radiating against them. He was sure Evan would open the suitcase to check and when he didn't, and they watched it drop into the lake and gurgle to the bottom, he felt relief.

Unaware that Evan had further plans for them, he thought he'd drop him off at the house and was shocked when he ordered him to drive the car and follow him in his rental. Tommy played the good little boy and did as requested. They drove to the top of a mountain range and Tommy was again ordered to do something he didn't want to. Evan demanded he light the car on fire. He didn't want to destroy Scarlett's car, which he wasn't even sure was actually hers or if it belonged to the people she was house sitting for.

Tommy struggled to light the match after Evan told him to poke a hole in the gas tank and stuff a pair of jeans beneath it. When the second match took, the fire spread quickly. Gasoline was an excellent accelerant. Evan and Tommy climbed into Evan's rental, and Tommy assumed they'd leave and he'd take him home, but then Evan pulled the car over, got out, and watched as the car exploded. The man was full of surprises.

Still thinking he'd drop him off at home. At that point it was wishful thinking. He wanted to get back to Scarlett, or home with his grandparents. His gramps was strict and cruel, but he knew what to expect. Instead, Evan drove him to his home in New Mexico — Poppy Hills. He texted Scarlett when they stopped for food, escaping to the restroom. Erring on the side of caution, in case Evan asked and demanded his phone, he erased every message and turned the phone off, stuffing it into his pants. If Evan didn't know he had it, he wouldn't ask for it.

Unable to sleep and wanting the memories to leave him, he sat up in bed, then trudged towards the steps. Eilida stood close to the sliding glass door, her back towards him. The step creaked beneath his foot as she spun her head around. Her small frame jumped and the plastic glass in her hand dropped to the floor, water spilled everywhere.

Catching her breath. "You scared me." She dropped her head and looked at the water puddled on the floor around her. "I'm sorry. I'll clean it up." She raced towards the kitchen. All that happened before Tommy could get a word out.

Rushing into the kitchen, he clutched her hand and drew her in to him. Small trembles emanated from her body. "I didn't mean to scare you."

She peered into his blue eyes. "It's not you, its storms. I was facing my fear."

Anger rose inside Tommy. He hated Evan for what he did to her and the other girls and their families. He hadn't decided if the dead ones were luckier than the victims Evan left alive. Chelsea Mora was an example. *If she hadn't suffered, would she have sought a boyfriend who was an abusive punk asshole?*

In the morning, Tommy woke, sunlight filtering through the curtains, not a sign of the previous night's storm. The sun's rays brought out warm highlights in Eilida's hair. She lay curled in the crook of his arm. Sliding over, careful not to shake the bed, he stood and showered. When he returned to the room, she stretched.

"Good morning."

She blinked her eyes against the balmy sunlight. "Good morning," she said in a small voice.

Her vulnerability made him desire her more. Her thick curls spread behind her head like a flower. Eyes dark as indigo, almost black. Gateways to her soul. Her tiny frame, perky boobs, and oval face, flawless. Outside she was the most beautiful woman he'd ever laid eyes on. Inside she was a tormented soul. One he may never really be afforded the chance to know. It wasn't that she didn't speak her mind, it was that she guarded her humanity.

She'd allowed him to take care of her and allowed him to friend her. *But would she allow him to speak the truth? Would the truth destroy her?* He mulled that thought over. If Evan hadn't destroyed her, then she was far stronger than he gave her credit for. It was time to tell her the story. Just as Scarlett told him her story as they sat in the cabin. She relayed the tale of her life, holding nothing back. Tonight, he'd tell her.

Tommy walked down the stairs, his long legs taking two at a time and strolled past her research, not giving it a glance as he grabbed his keys and left.

Tommy leaned over and stroked Eilida's hair from her face, giving her a long, sensual kiss. Then he pulled up and walked out the door. Eilida admired his round, firm ass. After he disappeared, she padded downstairs, grabbed a cup of coffee and eyed her piles of research. She couldn't leave all this over his living room floor and so decided she'd take it upstairs to the empty extra room. It'd be out of the way and she could work on it in quiet.

Refilling her coffee, she searched her phone for Alice Burkhalder's number. She was the kind of woman who was rough and hard on the outside but soft in the middle. They didn't know each other well, but she'd visited Eilida while she was recovering and gave her the night stick she kept tucked beneath her driver's seat as a gift after she was released. Alice is the woman Eilida thought of as her guardian angel.

The phone rang twice, then Alice's deep voice resonated through the speaker, "Hello, Eilida?" They'd exchanged numbers and she urged Eilida to call anytime. She'd been a very close friend of her parents.

Eilida smiled and they made small talk. Alice asked her about school and how she was doing, then Eilida jumped into her project and the research she'd unearthed.

"No charts were ever found, which really puzzled the police. Around his home they found astrology books, computer programs, but no charts," Alice said.

Eilida gave an audible sigh, and spied the picture of Tommy and his family on the top of the pile. "Do you remember a child born during Hurricane Chloe?"

She gave a light chuckle. "I do. He was the light during the night with his bald head and perfect little body. Dillon Findley. I kept up with him for a couple years until his family moved to South Carolina away from the beach area."

Eilida willed her mind to think about Tommy with a bald head and being tiny. The thought made her giggle. "I met him. We're friends."

"Well, I'll be damned," Burkhalder said in a shocked voice.

"We met a couple years ago at an astrology convention and I bumped into him here at the college. He doesn't know yet that his birthday is the day... He doesn't even know about my family. I glimpsed his wallet," Eilida said, picking up her coffee. Deception echoed inside her head as she thought of how he appeared at the same college. Was he here for her? Stop being paranoid, that's silly, she told herself, but the thought lingered.

The phone was silent for a minute, then Burkhalder spoke, "You're going to make a fine investigative reporter one day. Tell me the kind of man he's grown into."

"He's tall, muscular, has ice blue eyes, blond hair, and he's studying criminal justice."

"He sounds like more than a friend," voiced Burkhalder.

"I don't know. I feel safe around him, even though his birthday scares me," Eilida said, setting down her coffee and picking up the picture of Tommy and his family.

They continued their conversation and Eilida asked her about the other girls. The ones like her who were now adults.

Burkhalder froze and an eerie silence filled the airways between them. Alice finally broke the silence. "When they were little, I got a lot of phone calls hung up on me and doors slammed in my face. Now three of you are adults." She sighed. "You, Daisy and... Chelsea. You're the only one I've ever spoken to..."

Burkhalder's pause before Chelsea's name returned Eilida's mind back to the article she read last night — Mora, that was the last name. "Oh my. Not the same Chelsea Mora that was murdered?" The words dripped from her mouth.

"I'm afraid so, yes. It gave me a shock. Her funeral was only a few days ago."

Eilida gulped. "I didn't know her, but she was here. We were at the same school." Dread sunk into her gut and she clutched the pendant around her neck so hard it pinched the palm of her hand. Wild thoughts flew through her mind.

Was James Swan involved with Evan? Did he know him? She shook the thoughts away. James was a demented young man and he didn't murder her in the fashion Evan O'Conner used. But he was still on the loose.

Burkhalder soothed her and changed the subject; setting a date to get together after Thanksgiving. Hanging up the call, Eilida sat for a minute gathering her nerves. She then collected all her work and carried it upstairs to the extra room, laying it out on the floor.

She opened the door as she worked to allow the heat to warm up the room but it remained chilly, then she remembered the vent was closed. She peered upwards at it, then went downstairs and grabbed a chair from the kitchen table, but it was bulky so she sat it down, remembering he had a small ladder in the laundry room.

Lacing her arm through the curved bar, she hauled it upstairs. It was much lighter than the chair. She opened it up, positioning it beneath and to a slight left of the vent. She pushed against the lever, but it wouldn't budge.

She trudged downstairs again and into the garage. A small tool box sat on a work shelf jutting out from the wall. Sifting through its contents, she found a pair of pliers and a screwdriver. If the pliers didn't work she'd take the cover off.

Marching up the stairs and into the bedroom, she gripped the pliers onto the lever and pulled hard. She lost her footing and teetered on the ladder for a second before bracing her hands against the wall to halt her movement. Frustrated, she took the screwdriver and twisted away at the screws.

The moved, slow, and her arm ached as it twisted the screw above her head. She got one out, then shook her arm before starting on the other. The last screw dropped and she pulled the vent plate off. It didn't come easy as she tugged at it. The ache in her arms enough, she was ready to drop them to her sides, then it came off. A clear bag hung over the side of the open vent. She rested the vent plate on the ladder beside her feet and reached for the clear bag, forgetting about the aching in her arms.

It was a large freezer bag filled with papers. Curious, she unzipped it and pulled out the contents. Quickly unrolling them, she stared at a stack of papers rolled into the center of a map. She grabbed the stack of papers and stared at the map. It was of the U.S. with writing and dots across several southern states.

There were names. When she saw hers she dropped it, realizing what it was — a map of each of Evan O'Conner's kills.

The map floated to the ground as she unfurled the papers clutched in her hand — charts. Astrological charts with Evan's name on them, exactly what she wanted! The room spun in circles and she reached for the wall. *Why are these at Tommy's house?* was her last thought as she fainted, toppling off the ladder.

Escape

The humid air clung to her skin as Burkhalder walked up the steps of the small beach bungalow. Large tropical flowers surrounded it and lush green grass. She couldn't imagine how this couple acquired enough money to buy a beach home. She shrugged, assuming Evan O'Conner had provided well for them in his will. *Keeping secrets pays off*, she thought, knocking on the door.

A tall, thin man with a near bald head answered the door. "Mrs. Burkhalder, please come inside."

She didn't have the heart to correct him. She wasn't a Mrs. She and Frank decided against marrying, but if they had she'd be Mrs. Roy. Smiling, she entered the bungalow. "Good morning, Mr. Kurl."

A small, round woman brought out a tray with three glasses and a pitcher of sweet tea. "It's such a pleasure to meet you under better circumstances," she said, placing the tray on a wicker coffee table and pouring the tea.

Their backyard was the beach. A set of French doors were opened onto a screened room and the breeze from the sea blew into their home. Even a small home like this would cost a fortune.

"I could say the same," Burkhalder voiced, taking a seat on the flowered loveseat with a wicker base.

The woman handed her a glass and sat on a chair across from her. "Isn't it beautiful? We planned this for so many years."

"It is breathtaking and it's a pleasure to meet you again," said Burkhalder. She had no doubt the Kurls had earned their little piece of paradise. Working for Evan O'Conner Senior, then Junior, she could only imagine the horrific scenes they'd witnessed. Years ago, when Burkhalder and Frank discovered Evan owned Poppy Hills, they made a visit but couldn't get through the gates and made no headway with Evan. Mrs. Kurl seemed as though she wanted to talk but with her employer's watchful eye, and the fact that he was a sociopathic narcissist, Burkhalder understood the woman's silence.

Mr. Kurl piped in, "We know you're not here to see our dream home. You want to know about the O'Conners."

Down to business. She wondered how many officers and reporters had questioned them in the past year and a half. She scratched her eyebrow. "You're right." Lowering her hand, she placed it in her lap and gazed towards Mrs. Kurl, relaying her two and a half-decade search for the Hurricane Killer.

Mr. and Mrs. Kurl nodded in unison, then Mr. Kurl spoke, "We tried to stay out of the business of our employers. They paid us well and gave us a home." He paused for a second. "We also didn't want to know the details. It was safer for us and our boy that way. When Mr. O'Conner senior died, Mrs. O'Conner left soon after with her new man and his will provided well for us to maintain the home until his son was of age to take over. We never saw the boy again after she moved." He glanced toward his wife then back to Burkhalder. "We didn't want to. She wasn't a nice woman."

Burkhalder narrowed her eyes. "Can you give me an example?"

Mrs. Kurl shifted in her seat. "She didn't have nice words towards us, always complaining. After he died, she said he provided better for us than he did his own wife and child. And she never... bonded with baby Evan the way mothers do. She didn't nest, or have any motherly instincts, yet she admired the boy. It's difficult to find the words. It was almost as if she resented motherhood. Since new psychology has come out, I think the unexpected death of her husband brought on post-partum depression. But I'm no psychologist."

Mr. Kurl picked up the flow where Mrs. Kurl left off. "Mrs. O'Conner was a self-absorbed bitch."

Mrs. Kurl narrowed her eyes and scolded her husband, "Hal!"

He shrugged. "They're all dead. There's no need to be anything but candid."

Folding her hands in her lap Mrs. Kurl agreed, "I suppose you're right."

"Damn skippy I am!"

Burkhalder enjoyed the banter between the older couple and smiled wide. She wondered if one day that would be her and Frank. "Who owns the house now?"

The couple glanced at each other wide-eyed. "The only living relative to the second Mr. O'Conner," said Mrs. Kurl in a quiet voice.

"Who's that?"

Mrs. Kurl shifted in her seat again. "Scarlett Jones. She's Evan's biological aunt but..."

Burkhalder perked up with the mention of the name Scarlett. The elusive woman that somehow holds the key to the mystery. She didn't know how yet. But with the Kurls' unease, she thought maybe she'd finally find out.

Mr. Kurl picked up where Mrs. Kurl left off. "She was Mrs. O'Conner's biological sister and they looked so much alike. We never told anyone what we're going to tell you, including Evan number two. He tried to pry it out of us but we held fast to our guns that we knew nothing."

"You see, Scarlett came to stay with them for a short period of time. I wasn't allowed inside the house much during her stay but one afternoon they invited me in to clean and I saw something. I'm still not convinced what I saw was correct, but Philmonia's attitude toward baby Evan solidified for me that it was exactly what I thought."

She took in a deep breath and leaned forward as if relaying the biggest secret of the century. "I was cleaning upstairs, vacuuming, and Philmonia strolled out of her sister's room. I glanced into it as she shut the door. Scarlett had a baby bump, but so did Mrs. O'Conner. After she shut the door she turned a key and locked it then went into her own room and closed the door, but not all the way. I continued vacuuming in awe of what I saw and worked my way to the cracked door. Philmonia stood in front of a large mirror adjusting her baby bump. Pregnant women don't adjust their bellies."

Burkhalder's eyes widened. "Are you saying Philmonia wasn't Evan's biological mom but Scarlett is?"

"That's exactly what she's saying," said Mr. Kurl, answering her question.

From all the conversations Burkhalder had had over the years with anyone involved in the Hurricane Killer's life, this tidbit of info made perfect sense and wasn't a revelation to Burkhalder. Her and Frank had known for many years that Scarlett was most likely Evan's biological mother, since Frank snuck into the snaky lawyer's office and took pictures of Evan and Philmonia's DNA comparisons.

"You mentioned Evan knew about her?"

"Oh yes, but we don't think he knew much. One day, his hand wrapped in a bloodied shirt, he came to us with a picture of her. You see, Mr. Fritz – Mr. O'Conner senior's lawyer – had us take all his stuff and dump it somewhere. The safest place we could think of was the attic space above the garage. I locked the door and kept the key. Somehow Evan found the key and the room. I can only imagine what he thought of all the paraphernalia he found in the room," Mr. Kurl piped in.

"The first Mr. O'Conner and his wife were uh..." Mrs. Kurl paused for a second, "sexual freaks. It was never my place to question and I tried to keep my eyes and ears out of it. That was their private business."

Burkhalder already assumed Philmonia and hubby were sex freaks, since he died of a heart attack while tied to the bed, but hearing it from one who'd seen it in action cemented the thought in her head. Baby Evan grew up, reminded Philmonia of her sexually deviant husband, and she transferred the urges to her son. Philmonia's own father was a rapist who died a horrible death in prison, shanked by another inmate. She never had a chance. Burkhalder had a big heart, but felt little sympathy for anyone in that family. She'd seen the destruction and felt nothing but disgust for them.

Now Burkhalder needed to ask the question to gain the answer for the real reason she was there. "When Evan moved into his father's house, did he have anyone come over?"

Mr. Kurl snorted. "Friends. He preferred solitude and privacy but there was the young kid he moved in back in oh... 2010 maybe. At first the kid lived in one of the outer houses and he had him helping us with jobs around the grounds. But..."

Mrs. Kurl continued her husbands' thoughts. It tickled Burkhalder that this couple knew each other so well they could do that. "He moved him into the big house. That was a sign of affection coming from Evan. His feelings for the boy were evident in the way he watched him. His eyes brightened and smiled. He quit disappearing. Now we know the times he disappeared coincide with his... uh... crimes, but then we didn't know. He doted on the kid and I'd say, in his own way, loved him."

This was exactly what Burkhader was searching for. "Can you describe him for me?"

Mrs. Kurl jumped on answering the question. "Oh yes. He was a tall, gangly kid but after all that hard work his muscles filled out and his long blond hair he most times wore in a ponytail."

"Do you remember his name?" asked Burkhalder.

Mr. Kurl answered this one, "Tommy, just Tommy. We never got a last name or learned much about his past. He was as private, if not more so, as Mr. O'Conner."

Burkhalder cringed, she didn't think Evan deserved the respect of being called Mr. O'Conner. *Narcissistic Slime-worm* fit him better. "Thank you, I don't want to eat up any more of your time."

Everything was piecing together nicely. Evan killed his cousin, Emily Turnwell, under the assumption she was his half-sister and celebrated by taking the young man, Tommy, on a romantic getaway. *Did he kill Evan? Why?* The questions haunted her.

Evan took the kid in and, from the sounds of it, treated him like a king. Evan's death wasn't an act of passion but a calculated kill.

"It's been nice getting it off my chest. I hate carrying all that with me," said Mrs. Kurl.

Alice Burkhalder nodded as she rose from the wicker loveseat. Mr. and Mrs. Kurl walked her towards the door. On a table alongside the wall near the front door stood a grouping of pictures in boat-rope frames. They were tilted towards the living room and away from the door. The reason she'd missed them when she came in.

One picture caught her eye. A young man, tall and blond. His hair cut in a high and tight. In his hand he held a large catfish and had a wide smile on his face. Burkhalder stopped. A good investigator looked at all angles. If this kid was related to the Kurls than he was a suspect too. "You mentioned a son. Is this him?" she questioned, pointing to the frame.

Mr. Kurl's eyes twinkled. "No, that's our grandson. Strapping young man, isn't he?"

"He loves to fish. Since moving to Florida, we are close and he visits often. He and the mister take weekend fishing trips," Mrs. Kurl said with a smile.

"Nice looking young man. Did your son ever live with you at Poppy Hills?" *Was possible the young man sought his own vengeance?*

"Our son was a young pup when Mr. O'Conner Senior hired us and he stayed with us until he joined the Marines at eighteen. We did our best to keep him away from the main house and the O'Conners. I was relieved when he wrote us into the will, allowing us to stay on the property and maintain it, and Philmonia left," said Mrs. Kurl, her face wrinkled in a cringe.

"When young Evan moved in, we didn't have our son visit anymore. We didn't want our grandchild exposed to him. It was evident when we met him the first time that something wasn't right with him," said Mr. Kurl, shaking his head.

Burkhalder climbed into her Kia rental and headed towards the hotel, voice dialing Frank.

"Afternoon, Red," his deep voice resonated inside her ear. Burkhalder stopped at a red light.

"The Kurls gave me an earful, but first what did you find out about Fritz?" Frank was in New Mexico, investigating.

"Scarlett owns Poppy Hills now. I'm on my way there now. As for Fritz, he retired and fled the country with a boatload of money soon after signing the house over to her. I'm guessing she paid him off."

That sounded shady, but she expected nothing less from the slimy self-serving lawyer.

"Kurls have anything to offer?" he asked.

"Yes. They confirmed Scarlett is most likely his mother. They also have a grandson. He fits the description of the kid you saw him with in Salvation Cove, only his hair is short."

The light turned green and Burkhalder crawled into the intersection. A car to her left ran the red light, plowing into the passenger side of her car, throwing the vehicle into the opposite lane of oncoming traffic. Brakes squealed and the sound of crushing metal filled Frank's ears.

"Alice, honey!" he screamed into the phone.

She didn't hear it as she was knocked out upon impact. The airbag rose and surrounded her unconscious body.

And the Clock Struck Midnight

Tommy had reconsidered before confronting Eilida. He needed courage in a bottle. He'd never been this nervous in his life. When he met Evan it scared the piss out of him and he sweated a few times but stayed calm on the outside. Eilida was something different. He was attracted to her in a way he'd never felt and couldn't explain.

Maroon 5 *Maps* played in the background. He'd heard the song hundreds of times without ever really hearing the lyrics.

So I'm following the map that leads to you

The map that leads to you
Ain't nothing I can do
The map that leads to you

He stopped cold, holding a beer to his lips. Maps — that was it. Their life maps placed them together. His meeting Scarlett wasn't coincidence. His being born during Hurricane Chloe wasn't a coincidence. His relationship with Eilida and with Evan — none of it coincidences. It was a grand design beyond anyone's control.

Evan's maps and charts flashed through his head. Plunging the needle into Evan's neck and holding the blade he'd used to slaughter his own family was all planned. The stars and planets dictated it. All the answers were in those damn charts that he couldn't read. When he'd tried, his stomach bubbled and his lunch rose into his throat. He'd pushed it down and rolled everything together and kept it hidden.

With a sudden urge to get home, and a curiosity to finally read the charts and understand what was hidden inside them, he jumped off the bar stool he'd been warming. Tossing a twenty at the edge of the bar, he took a deep breath then strolled to the door and walked outside into the chilly air.

His senses were dulled just enough that he wasn't drunk yet and was ready to confront demons — no more hiding in the shadows. He pulled into his driveway, but Eilida's car was gone. His heart sank as he rushed toward the door. Newly fallen leaves crunched beneath his boots.

His gut numb with worry. He knew his reaction wasn't reasonable and that she probably just went out for a minute but he couldn't fight off the overwhelming sensation that something was terribly wrong. Throwing his front door open he spied the living room and rushed into the kitchen, then the bathroom. Everything looked normal, except her research was gone.

Siding with caution, he grasped the handle of his blade and traipsed up the stairs. On first sight, his bedroom door was open and looked as he'd left it. Then he noted the empty guestroom door was ajar and his heart drummed against his chest. Stalking toward the open door, he pushed it open all the way. Standing in the doorway, he laid eyes on his ladder beneath the vent and noted the vent cover on the floor. A screwdriver and pliers lay beside it at the door.

Helplessness seared through his body like fire and he screamed into the air, "No!" then rushed down the steps, taking them two at a time. He flew past the coffee table, the wind caused by his rush lifted a paper off it and it glided to the floor in front of him. Catching his eye, he paused and lifted it up. A picture of his parents holding him as a baby stared at him. He stared back in awe and shock, grasping his ponytail with his other hand. Sick to his stomach, he sank onto the couch and murmured, "I'm sorry Eilida. I didn't want you to find any of this out. Not this way. I'm sorry." A tear slid from his eye and dropped onto the picture.

Gathering himself, he knew what he had to do and headed towards Eilida's, hoping she'd gone home. When he arrived at her apartment complex, relief filled his heart as he spotted her car outside. Tommy placed his sheathed blade into the glove box and exited his truck.

Voices behind him caught his attention and he turned to see a young couple with their dog leaving the wooded trail. They walked past Tommy and the woman shot him a quick smile before she turned to wrap her arm around the man. Tommy nodded acknowledgement but kept a poker face. He'd grown used to women smiling and flirting even in the presence of their spouses.

Straightening his back, he lifted his hand to knock on her door but paused, collecting his courage. He knocked and listened as footsteps padded closer to the door.

"Go the fuck away!" came through the door.

He expected and deserved that. "Eilida, just let me in. I can explain it all."

"I said go away!"

"I can't, you need to know."

He stood at the door listening to silence for a few minutes, then turned on his heel, defeated. She'd come around, he told himself. He'd have to practice patience and wait her out. Turning the corner of her building he heard a deadbolt unlock and a door creak open. Glancing over his shoulder, Eilida stood in the entranceway peering at him through narrowed eyes.

Her hair mussed, eyes reddened, and cheeks stained by tears, but still as beautiful as ever, he turned to face her. "I'm sorry," he said, his expression stoic and flat and his voice shaky.

She took a step backwards and inside her apartment, leaving the door open. He walked towards the doorway and stopped at the entrance. She sat on her sofa, the map and charts laid out on the floor in front of her. Cautiously, he stepped through the doorway and closed the door behind him. He stood speechless with his thumbs in his pockets, unable to control his wandering eyes, admiring her ensemble. She didn't have a bra on and her nipples had hardened from the chilly air. Each curve of her body was highlighted beneath the thermals that hugged it. He felt himself stiffening inside his pants.

"I was at *Flashers* and realized today that I need to tell you everything. I rushed home and you weren't there." He shifted on his feet. "I care so much about you I've... been scared. I don't want to lose you."

Her eyes still narrowed, she said with disdain, "Don't stop there."

He took a few steps towards her. "Can I?" he asked, pointing to the seat beside her on the sofa.

"I'd rather you didn't. You can take a seat at the table," she said, picking up a large hammer lying beside her on the couch. "Don't make me use this, because I will."

He nodded, glancing at the hammer, then noting a bag of ice on the table beside him. He took a few steps backward and sat on one of the kitchen table chairs beginning his story, starting with the day he found his best friend, Mark, dead and his meeting Scarlett, but he left several details out. He dreaded her reaction towards him and being shoved out of her life.

The fact that Tommy had never hurt Eilida and she'd felt safe in his presence were the only reasons she let him in her apartment. Well, not the only reasons. She was curious, and pushed the anger and fear inside her down. She'd hear him out before pushing him out of her life completely.

She listened intently as he spoke. He flipped the chair backwards and sat down, resting his arms on the backrest. The way kids sit in junior high because they think they're cool. His expression flat, almost too flat, like he was struggling to keep his emotions under control. Every so often he'd lose control and flinch. She said nothing as she soaked up his words in disbelief.

It was all too perfect. He happens to walk in and catch creepy Evan raping his best friend Mark's father's girlfriend. Conveniently there's a paperweight on the dresser that he smashes against the skull of the unsuspecting monster. Scared, he runs from the house and only stops when his conscience gets the better of him and he thinks to call the police. Instead, a mysterious woman appears and he follows her back to her home. It was more like she waited for him.

The two form a friendship and plot against Evan and convenience plays out again. They trick him into thinking Tommy killed his own mother and he assisted Tommy with dumping the body that's really a suitcase loaded with bricks wrapped in a comforter. Evan, thinking he's saved Tommy, takes him home with him where Tommy stays for a short time, long enough to find all the evidence in front of her.

Patrice's words and interpretation of Tommy's chart filled Eilida's thoughts. *Jupiter is the other planet in this grouping. Jupiter expands, exaggerates and inflates what he touches, while Virgo can be critical, picky, perfectionistic and judgmental. This combination is often troublesome. The 8th house, where Jupiter resides, has a bad reputation since it contains such things as death, rebirth, sex, debt, intense experiences, things you suppress, transformations and shared resources. This placement implies he'll experience extremely intense events and situations, some of which will be of his own doing, since Jupiter is part of that triad with his Sun which represents him at the core, and Mars which demands action. Mars, in turn, is connected to Uranus in the 12th, which suggest impulsive promptings to act from his subconscious. Thus, he may take action on a traumatic experience in an inappropriate manner.'* The part about intense events that may be his doing explained the situation better than Tommy could with words.

Eilida twisted her lips, racking her brain to remember everything Patrice had said. *In spite of the conservative and responsible impression he gives, most of that is only in appearance. There's a lot of emotion brewing beneath the surface which may not always be based on reality. His emotions will easily overrule his common sense. In spite of the conservative and responsible impression he gives, most of that is only on the surface.'*

He still hadn't answered how he'd acquired all creepy Evan's charts. "How did you get all this?" she asked, her voice flat.

"I went back to his house after his death. The housekeeper let me in. She remembered me."

That didn't add up. The housekeeper just let him in? More of Patrice's words floated to the front of her brain. *There's another caution flag on his chart with Neptune, the planet of deception, conjunct his ascendant. This implies that people will not see him as he really is.'* Deception! The deception that kept eating at her. *'He could also be delusional to a certain degree, though being in Capricorn helps a little. Nonetheless, Neptune is opposite his Moon, so will affect his emotions. He may react emotionally in ways that are unrealistic that derive from his subconscious.'* Delusional, unrealistic, yup that summed up his explanations so far.

"Why would she do that?" she asked.

"I told her I was there for a visit."

Now his story really didn't add up. "But that was years later."

He nodded and dropped his head. "I visited on and off."

"You stayed with this evil man more than once?!"

He nodded. "I wanted proof, physical proof, that he was the Hurricane Killer. A weapon or something. I grasped at straws."

Eilida doubted the story, although the intensity in Tommy's eyes showed no lies. He told her the truth as he knew it and couldn't see the truth for what it was. He didn't design the master plan; he was merely a pawn. A chill ran up her spine and a cool breeze swept over her.

She shuddered. "Do you hear yourself?" she asked.

He sat back, his hands clutching the back of the chair. "It's haunted me and played through my head long enough. That's how it happened."

She didn't think him guilty of any crime other than emotional stupidity. "Did it ever occur to you how *conveniently* everything worked out?"

He narrowed his eyes. "What do you mean?"

"You just happen to run into this woman and the two of you concoct a plan to get close enough to Mr. Creepy to pin him to the murders, yet look at my floor. You had the evidence, yet you hid it. All this," she pointed to the mass of papers, "if you'd turned that in the Turnwells might still be alive! I wouldn't have hit my head and spent a year in therapy!"

Oh crap! she thought. Patrice said he was a meticulous planner when he wanted something. *'Another closed loop aspect on his chart involves that smaller triangle with just the green lines. That is called a sextile pattern and often indicates a talent or ability. His Sun is at the apex, which indicates those other planets are supporting what he wants. Mars is one of them, in his 4th house which includes endings and new beginnings, his past, cultural roots and home environment. He's in Taurus, where Mars is in his ancient debility, but that doesn't actually cause a problem. Mars tends to be impulsive and act first, think later, but in Taurus it lends patience and determination to achieve what he wants. It can channel Mars' drive and aggression in a slow, methodical way. Thus, when he is working on something that means a lot to him, he will have patience to pursue it as long as necessary to achieve what he wants.'*

He gulped. "You also might not have your memories!" he snapped, "and all that *evidence* doesn't pin him to anything. It's all circumstantial."

Her chest heaved with a large sigh. He was right. It was her memories that pinned him as the Hurricane Killer. The evidence in front of her wouldn't have cemented the case. She believed his end of the story. Like her, he was a child victim that "bought" into a world his inner Cancer desired.

She glanced at the shark tooth hanging on a cord around his neck. It bobbed against her chest during sex but she'd never asked its significance.

He stood and walked towards her, kneeling in front of her. Grasping her free hand, her other hand still clutching the hammer, he searched her eyes. "I'm sorry."

She lay the hammer on the couch beside her. She felt only empathy for him. He'd lost his best friend and was impressionable, scared, and vulnerable. The same as her. This anonymous woman offered him a story he wanted to believe.

"What's this?" she asked, leaning toward him and lifting the leather cord around his neck.

"A shark's tooth. When I was a kid, before my parents died, my mother used to collect them from the beach. It's my way of keeping them close now that they're gone."

Eilida's eyes drifted to the floor. "I was orphaned so young I barely remember mine, but my aunt and uncle adopted me. They're good parents."

"My grandparents took me in. I was fifteen. A plane crash. I was at summer camp when my grandparents picked me up and brought me home with them." His ice blue eyes filled with sadness.

Eilida's blue eyes searched his face as though they were looking for something beyond the surface. She sensed him stiffen, as if she'd suck the secrets from him.

The death of his parents and best friend, coupled together with his actions, made perfect sense. Ms. Clandestine, Scarlett, took the places in his life of those he'd lost. She preyed on his weak, mourning heart. Another aspect of his chart: *Following your heart is usually a good thing, but he may not always do so in a positive way. What he wants he'll pursue. He won't always see things as they really are, at least as far as social norms are concerned.'*

"I'm sorry. I don't think this woman had your best interests at heart. She preyed on your weakness and dropped you into a dangerous world. The stuff my nightmares are made of." He was a distraught teenager, grieving over the loss of his family. She understood his actions.

She felt the heat rising in her as they talked and flirted, getting closer with each word until their lips met and their tongues mingled. He snaked his hands beneath her shirt and drew her on top of him as he leaned backwards against the arm of the couch. Tingles ran across her spine. She wanted him more than anything.

A ting of warning shot through her, but desire soon covered it over as she melted in his firm arms and allowed his warm tongue inside her mouth.

She sat on top of him. The only thing separating them was clothing. His kisses trailed across her neck, behind her ears, then back to her mouth. He lifted her top over her head, thick dark waves trailed from it as he pulled it off and tossed it.

She scooted backwards and unbuckled his belt, moving to the button

165

on his jeans then, grasping the zipper between her fingers, she pulled it down. Sliding her hands into his pants, she grabbed his thick, full shaft and stroked gently.

He moaned, slipping his hand underneath her thermal bottoms and rubbed against her salivating clit. She felt it throbbing against his fingers. Taking his time, driving her wild, he continued past and inside her, keeping one finger against her clit. She was on the verge of an orgasm when he first slid his cock inside her. The foreplay drove her to the point of ecstasy and she felt her vagina squeezing him as she erupted.

The temperature in the room went up several degrees as they indulged in passionate, lust-filled sex. Over and over, they entwined together on her couch and finally settled on the carpet. Once they exhausted their youthful energy, they lay on the floor. Eilida's leg tangled beneath Tommy's. Each had a mouthful of words to speak to the other.

She sat up, an elbow on the floor, and perched her head against her palm, soaking in his beautiful sculpted face.

He twisted one of her thick locks in his hand. "Everything is OK now."

The words echoed inside her head, begging her to remember

something, but what? She looked towards her kitchen counter and Sandy, her childhood monkey, taken hostage by the asshole who killed her family. His black eyes stared at her and begged for her to remember something. She sighed and laid her head against the floor. "How do you know that?"

As the words left her mouth, he lifted his torso upwards and peered into her eyes. The feeling overwhelmed her. The same feeling that shot through her the times he'd 'saved' her from harm.

Every hair on her body stood at attention when memories from her delusions swarmed her. She finally understood her feelings for him and the safe feeling he brought her. She was at the peak of her feverish frenzy when the very same words were spoken while depositing Sandy at her bedside then everything else followed. A blond man in an elevator. But it wasn't, it was a blond man at her bedside! "You!" She shot upward and stood above him.

"You, how… Oh, your uncle." She remembered the astrology convention and the creepy sensation she kept feeling that wouldn't go away. Tommy lived in New Mexico with his uncle. His uncle was the monster who'd killed her family! Then the disappearing

ring and an identical ring turning up on the monster, Evan's, death bed. She was one of a few people who knew that and he wouldn't expect that she knew. He'd stolen the ring and given it to Evan. *But was Evan the monster really his uncle?* Putting two and two together, her deep blue eyes shot at him. "He's wasn't your uncle, it was the monster! No, this, this can't. Get out of here!" She shouted at him, grabbing his clothes and throwing them at him. "Get!"

She wasn't completely sure what her mind put together, but his eyes... she remembered them from the hospital. He'd brought her Sandy. Even though she'd been in a coma at the time, she now recognized them. So she logically deduced if he'd brought Sandy, and she'd last seen Sandy in the hands of Evan, then Tommy knew him. That idea brought her full circle to his "uncle" — the one he talked about, but she never met, at the astrology convention. And then the ring. It was her ring. It had disappeared after her and Sage hung out with him. Anger burned inside her and she wanted him out of her life!

"There's more. You need to hear it all." He stood, grasping at his clothes as they flew past him.

His comment confirmed her suspicions. "I don't need to hear shit!" she screamed, not caring if her neighbors heard.

He grabbed her arms. "Eilida, this is not what you might think. It's more complicated. I'm a victim, same as you."

She brushed his hands from her arms as if they were pesky bugs and pushed him toward the front door. "Get the fuck out and don't ever come back!" She didn't care if James Swan was on the loose. He didn't scare her near as much as the monster! With that, she opened the door and pushed him into the cold — naked — and slammed and bolted the door behind him.

Unfortunate Accident

Within hours, Frank was at Burkhalder's bedside. Her hand cupped inside his as he leaned his elbows on the side of the mattress. She suffered a fair amount of bruising but no internal injuries. The airbag saved her life.

Her left arm in a splint as it suffered small fractures throughout, and a slight concussion, but that was her worst injury thanks to the airbag. This woman, her long fiery hair spilling on the pillow beneath her head, was the love of his life. Frank admired her pointed nose and fine features. Moving her hand to his mouth, he caressed his lips against it.

In the hallway, he heard a familiar voice nearing the room. He stood and stepped into the hallway. A blond woman rushed towards him and they embraced. Their arms folded around each other, he kissed the top of her head as tears streamed from her eyes, soaking into his shirt.

"She's... she's... going... to be... OK?" the woman said as more of a question than a statement through shallow breaths.

Frank nodded. "Yes. She's still knocked out from anesthetics but should be waking soon."

The blond woman, Talla, Frank's niece who he'd raised since she was a teen after her parents' death, loved Burkhalder since they day they found her in the woods. The woman had grown on her and brought out a spark in her uncle that lightened each step he took and kept a smile on his face.

The couple walked into the hospital room, an arm snaked around the other's back. Alice's eyes opened a crack and a crooked smile formed on her face.

Talla rushed to her side. "I was so scared. Don't you ever do that again," she said, kissing Burkhalder's cheek.

Alice couldn't halt her spreading smile, even when it caused a dull ache in her head. Waking up to her two favorite people was more than she could have asked.

"We need you. My kids need you," said Talla.

Frank joined the women at the bed. The love of his life. She was a stubborn, independent woman and at that moment he realized he didn't ever want to live his life without her. They'd been through plenty together, but nothing life threatening. When she was better, he'd put a ring on her finger and ask her to marry him.

Burkhalder lifted her head, but the pounding inside it made the feat of sitting up difficult. Frank slid his arm along her back and lifted, while Talla stuffed a couple pillows behind her.

"Did you get to Poppy Hills?"

Frank smiled. He didn't care about Poppy Hills. His concern was for her. He'd whipped the car around and headed straight for the airport, taking the first flight he could get on. But Alice was Alice and one-track-minded.

He nodded with a dimpled smile. "I didn't make it to Poppy Hills. You're more important."

"The Kurls have a son; a Marine, and a grandson," Burkhalder said, scrunching her face in pain.

"So you mentioned. We'll sort through that later. Right now it's not important." He kissed her head then pushed the nurse button on the contraption attached by a cord to the bed. He observed her wincing from pain. She needed more meds.

Three hours later, Frank stood outside the hospital wearing a grave expression. He'd already called in a favor. His phone to his ear. "Thanks," he said, pushing the red end button. He'd wait until she was feeling better and on the mend. If he mentioned the Kurls' son, Devlin, wasn't the only Marine in the family — their grandson Jenson followed in his father's footsteps, taking it one step further as an elite Marine Raider — she'd be out of bed and working.

He'd check for an alibi first.

"What's that?" asked a young teen with curly, short brown hair, spotting a blue lump between two large rocks along the shoreline.

Another teen squinted her eyes. "Where?" she asked, squinting her eyes further. She'd forgotten to put her contacts in and only saw fuzz from the distance.

"Between those rocks." The brown-haired girl moved closer. Noting the blue, she saw was a pair of jeans. She stopped, her mind processing the denim lump. Then she moved closer, one slow step at a time, swallowing hard. As she drew closer, her heart beat faster.

The blond followed in curiosity. "What is it?"

The brunette didn't speak and moved to the side of one of the rocks to get a better view. *Thump thump*, her heart beat against her chest. Her mind processing the blue lump. It had form and feet and shoes. She screamed loud enough to shatter glass.

The blond rushed towards her and froze when she stood close enough to see what her friend was screaming over. James Swan lay trapped between the rocks. His face battered, but not enough she didn't recognize it from the news. She grasped her screaming friend's hand and pulled her backwards toward her, then slid her phone out of her pocket and dialed 911.

Thanksgiving

Tommy couldn't stop thinking about Eilida. Scarlett was on her way over, only he didn't want to see her and had no urge to finish cooking the turkey in the oven. It was his fault, not hers, but now he'd lost Eilida. He couldn't stomach that and a huge hole ached inside his chest. He needed to make things right with her.

The doorbell rang, his heart lurched inside his chest. When he got to the door, Scarlett stood on the other side with wine and store-bought au gratin potatoes. He opened the door without a word and trudged back to the kitchen.

"She'll come around. The girl is tougher than you give her credit for." Her words did little to comfort him.

She shifted on her three inch heels, opened her mouth, then closed it when Tommy flashed her a disdainful look. His eyes narrowed, small lines causing crevices in his forehead. His ice blue eyes gray and void of their usual sparkle.

Always so sure of herself and confident, he'd never seen her nervous until now. She moved toward him, placing her hand against his back.

He shifted his torso and took a step away from her. "Don't touch me."

She nodded, moved her hand to her side and left the kitchen. When she noticed him setting the food on the table she joined and helped. Neither said a word. She'd pushed him too far, too fast. Always strong and determined, she'd forgotten that he wasn't a machine but an emotional young man who cared deeply about the world and Eilida. He wanted to right the wrongs in the world, especially Evan's.

They sat without words for several minutes before Scarlett broke the silence. "I'm sorry."

He glowered at her from across the table. "The hell you are!" He stood, walked towards the door, and grabbed his keys off the table.

"Where are you going?" she asked.

"None of your business," he said as he threw the door open and marched to his Lexus. He was done listening to her and her selfish motives.

Eilida set her phone down. She'd called her aunt and uncle, Sage, and tried Jay but he didn't answer. Leaving a message, she continued working on her report. Overcoming her fears, she sifted through Evan's charts, stopping to type on her computer. A knock on the door startled her and she jumped, her computer nearly falling off her lap. She caught her arm beneath it just before it flew off her lap.

Rising from her spot on the floor, she edged cautiously toward the door. The only person she could think would be knocking was Tommy, and she didn't want to see him. Lifting her feet off the ground, she peered through the peephole. Her face lit up as she unlocked and threw the door open, folding Jay into her arms.

His body against hers felt like her favorite pair of jeans against her skin, comfortable and perfect. "I'm so glad you're here." She squeezed him against her.

He welcomed her embrace and lifted her chin off his chest, placing his lips on hers, then sunk his tongue deep inside her mouth. The chilly air rushed at them but didn't faze either of them as they stood in a hearty kiss, their bodies radiating heat against the other.

He lifted her upward and she wrapped her legs around his waist, their mouths still deep in the kiss. With his foot, he closed the door behind them, and placed her down on the table. Tearing at each other's clothes, they stripped each other's pants off. He rubbed his cock along her clit, feeling the excitement rising inside himself. She grew wet and soaked the head of his hard cock.

He continued rubbing against her as he pushed up her shirt while licking around her areola. She leaned backward, her hands grasping his thick, hungry manhood, pushing it against her, desperate to feel his warmth inside her.

He teased, driving her into a frenzy as she kissed behind his ears and ran her empty hand through his brown locks, grasping a handful when he thrust inside her. Moans escaped her mouth. She missed this, and him. It was more than sex. It was Jay.

With so long between couplings, within minutes they reached ecstasy and released in unison. She thought of Tommy, how good it had felt, but it didn't compare to what she experienced with Jay. With Tommy it was lust and need, with Jay it was... love. The moment she realized that was a huge epiphany.

She was in love with the man who now smoothed her hair and dropped kisses along her cheek.

He rose and slipped his pants on. "I'm going to get my bag."

A wide smile stretched across her face as she watched him exit her apartment. She slipped her sweatpants on and tidied up her research.

Tommy pulled into a parking space outside Eilida's complex and stepped out of his truck, walking past a young, dark-haired man. Most days he might have said something in greeting, but today he was too distraught for casual conversation. He walked the path to her apartment. Rounding the corner, he knocked on her door.

"It's open," sounded Eilida's voice from inside. Shocked she'd be so ready to invite him in, he slowly opened the door. She was bent over, stacking all her files and notes.

"Eilida?"

She froze, then turned, rising gradually. Her eyes fixed on him. He wasn't who she was expecting. Sensing her unease, he moved inside sluggishly, not wanting to alarm her further.

Footsteps sounded against the paved walkway, halting outside the door. Both men's eyes shifted towards each other, then Eilida.

It sunk in that Eilida was never Tommy's. The look on her face; horror combined with sadness, said this other man was the man she belonged to.

The dark-haired man spoke after seconds of eerie silence, "E. what's going on?"

She stammered and dropped her eyes, unable to look him in the eye. "I'm sorry." She shifted her pleading eyes toward the man.

His eyes glanced toward Tommy again, filled with daggers, then at Eilida. The daggers replaced with hurt; understanding Eilida hadn't been faithful.

"This is why you couldn't come home for Thanksgiving. You tossed me to the side for him. He's all yours," he sneered, hefting his bag over his shoulder and leaving.

Tommy exploded inside watching Eilida crumple to the floor. He expected to come over and plead for her forgiveness, not find her with a boyfriend he hadn't known she had. All he wanted to do was hold her in his arms and make her world whole, but he'd destroyed it on so many levels. He stood glued to the spot where he was standing, and watched tears roll down her cheeks and drop onto her shirt.

Her head buried in her hands, he scanned the room and noted a tissue box on the counter beside her beloved stuffed monkey. Grabbing the entire box, he walked up beside her and kneeled down, lifting her face with one hand. He dabbed at her tears with his free hand.

At that moment, it didn't matter to him that he wasn't the man, it only mattered that he make it right. After several minutes, she rested her head against his chest. He smoothed back her hair, matted and tangled against her cheeks.

Eilida's eyes glazed over, stared blankly. In a whisper she said, "Was he your uncle?"

Bewildered and taken aback, he asked, "Who?"

"The monster," she said in ragged breaths.

"No, he wasn't," he responded, turning his eyes from her.

Dead is Dead

Burkhalder sat dressed in her bed watching the morning news, sipping on orange juice. Frank at her side, waiting on the discharge papers. Scrolling across the screen was *Man hunt over. James Swan, suspect in the Chelsea Mora case, body found yesterday.*

Her eyes enlarged and she tapped Frank who was leaned over, plugging her phone into the closest outlet. "What did I miss?"

"James Swan was found. He's dead..." She flipped through the channels, searching for another carrying the story. After running past each one, she turned it back and waited impatiently. North Carolina news wasn't important in Florida, but after approximately an hour they covered the story. Two teen girls found his body wedged between two rocks in Wicker's Creek.

Other than postmortem bruises, his body showed no signs of trauma. At this point the authorities were calling it a suicide.

"Doesn't that creek feed from a smaller creek close to the college?" she asked.

Frank rubbed his beard in thought, then reached for his phone and looked it up. He spread the map out and placed it in front of Burkhalder. "You know your geography. Look, there's a bike path goes over the water. It's secluded, could be where he jumped." *Or was pushed.* But he kept that to himself as he didn't want her worked up and investigating while she was recovering.

The sun streamed through the window as they woke. He'd held her all night as they watched movies then passed out. He wasn't sure why she'd let him stay, but wasn't going to ask. Tommy sitting with his back against the couch, legs stretched in front of him and Eilida with her head in his lap. She lifted up and rested on the couch beside him, stretching her arms and legs to work out the kinks. Her phone blinked from the table beside her. She grabbed it, hoping for a message from Jay. Her smile from the anticipation turned into a frown when she saw it wasn't him.

After a shower and homemade breakfast, compliments of Tommy, she called Burkhalder. Her excitement bubbling over.

"Hello," answered a male voice.

Wrinkling her nose in surprise and double checking the number, she asked, "Can I speak with Alice Burkhalder?"

"Ah… she's not available right now." She heard movement and then a quiet door creak.

"This is uh… Eilida. We were meeting up today…" she said with anticipation in her voice.

"She's been in an accident. Luckily, the air bags did their trick and she's recovering in the hospital, but won't be meeting you today. She's resting at the moment."

Shocked at the words. She'd always considered Burkhalder tough and strong. It never crossed her mind everyone can be broken. "I send her my prayers and wish her a speedy recovery."

"I'll give her your wishes and have her contact you once she's feeling better."

"Thank you." Eilida hung up the phone and stared at the floor in disbelief. Burkhalder, the woman who saved her from the arms of the monster, was in a hospital. Her heart went out to her.

"What's wrong?" asked Tommy from behind her as he stepped into the living room, towel-drying his hair.

Eilida tilted her head towards him, heat radiating through her body as he wore only a towel around his waist. She shook the thought and looked away. She didn't want to give anything away, and deceiving people wasn't her area of strength. "Uh… a friend was in an accident." Her plan, and the reason she allowed Tommy to stay overnight was to bring Tommy with her.

His eyes widened. "Are they OK?"

She nodded but said nothing else.

He shook his head once, then stepped back into the bathroom and dressed. When he returned, Eilida had the news on and sat stock still as she stared at the screen.

He froze when he saw James Swan's picture and the creek where his body was found. After getting James drunk, he took him to the path and the walking bridge. He lied and told James he was meeting his hook-up there. While they waited, they talked. Tommy accused him of killing his girlfriend, unsheathed the knife housed against his waist and walked toward him.

James' eyes widened and he turned to run but had backed against the edge of the bridge. Instead of running, he lost his footing and toppled over the edge. Tommy hadn't meant for him to die, but he hadn't felt any remorse either. James admitted to all of it, begging and pleading with Tommy once he saw the shiny blade.

An involuntary shudder swarmed Tommy's body. His eyes left the TV and shifted to Eilida who sat watching him, her eyes narrowed.

"He's been dead several days," she said, a notch above a whisper.

Tommy wasn't about to mention his involvement to Eilida. "How'd he die?"

"Suicide, they think. There's no signs of a struggle or fight." She stood, folding her arms, giving him the illusion she didn't believe it was suicide. Or maybe he was just being paranoid.

"I can't say I'm sorry. If he killed his girlfriend then its karma." He gave her something to mull over. It might well have been karma that killed Evan too.

One can only cause so much harm before something befalls them.

Eilida smirked. "Thanks for helping me." She twisted her lips. "I'm going to visit my friend today. Maybe we can catch up later?" The way she twirled her hair, he'd come to know that meant she was nervous and he doubted she was truly on her way to visit her friend, but what was she really up to?

Frank hung up with Eilida and hadn't taken two steps when his phone buzzed inside his pocket. He swapped the phones, looked at the ID, and answered.

"What did you find?" a touch of apprehension in his voice.

"I don't think Jenson Kurl is your man. He was on a confidential assignment May 8, 2014. His record is blacked out. My clearance won't get me any further through that door," sounded the deep voice.

Frank pulled at his beard. "It's not him. Thanks!"

He hung up and slipped back into Alice's room and grabbed the rest of her

stuff while she waited for the wheelchair
to bring her to the doors.

Patience is a Virtue

Tommy didn't believe Eilida. Her behavior changed and she nearly booted him out of her place. He wanted nothing more than for her to trust him and he'd given her enough, was the shoulder she cried on, yet she still didn't trust him. He eased his rented white Subaru Impreza into the apartment complex and wove around it. Her car was still in its spot, meaning she hadn't left.

He parked in an adjacent lot and strolled to her car, pulling the black baseball cap down over his forehead.

His eyes shifting to her apartment and seeing her window coverings closed, he walked past and towards her car. The day was overcast with thick, full stratus clouds and calling for snow in the higher elevations. Moving past her car at a slow pace, in one smooth movement he tucked a small GPS device beneath the passenger side mirror and continued walking.

She weaved through the city, finally getting onto US-17 N. It crossed his mind that maybe he was wrong and she was truly on her way to visit her friend, but the sensation in his gut said otherwise. They continued to head north and he made sure several cars stayed between them. Once she merged onto NC-12 he knew exactly where she was headed, but couldn't for the life of him understand why.

Eilida packed a small overnight bag in case her meeting took longer than she thought. It was a four-hour drive and weather conditions weren't favorable. In fact, the newscasters were calling for snow, although in the mountains not the coastal regions. She wasn't taking any chances. Tossing her bag into the back seat of her car, she fired the engine and cruised out of the parking lot.

Never had she visited the small town she and Tommy were born in. But she wasn't going for memories' sake. She remembered Burkhalder mentioning a deputy by the name of Jackson. Luckily for her, he was still there and was now the Sheriff of the small island town. He agreed to meet with her. Inside, her guts twisted with anticipation and she took deep breaths to calm herself.

North Carolina, always such a beautiful state, was barren of the usual green. The trees stood naked as if baring their deepest secrets. She whizzed past one after the other and unrolled her window a thumb's width when she headed over the Falen Sound. Chilly, salty air filled her lungs. No matter how many years passed, she'd never forget the scents of her birth place.

Most of the homes were empty during the winter months. Spring through summer brought in the tourists and snow birds. Prickles ran up her spine as she drove by the spot her birth home had stood. A new home took its place. It looked nothing like the one she barely remembered. Her last recollection of Billows Hollow was the monster pulling her out of the chest and the fiery red-headed cop, Burkhalder, taking her within her arms and to the shelter.

Her home close to the shore, she circled back to the main town. A tiny white car, several car lengths behind, caught her eye. She couldn't get a look at the driver since the car was too far away and tried to brush off the creepy feeling that ate at her insides. Swallowing hard, she took her eyes off the car and continued.

Every so often, she diverted her eyes to the road behind her and the little car was still there. There was only one main road, so it really had nowhere else to go. She turned off the main road towards the police station and the white car continued forward. Sighing relief, she got out of the car and ran into the police station.

The place was tiny, with a main room and a couple offices divided by a counter with a flip top for people to come and go. An older woman, her hair reminding her of a cotton ball, sat behind the counter.

"Can I help you?" she asked in a friendly voice.

"Yes." Eilida bit her lip. "I'm here to see Sheriff Martin."

The older woman, who had a name tag that read *MaddyJo* answered, small lines cracked across her forehead and webbed the corners of her eyes as she talked. "I'll get him."

She lifted herself off the stool she'd been sitting on and waltzed towards a door marked *Sheriff Martin*, her flowing skirt swayed side to side. She raised her arm to knock but a gentleman opened it before she had the chance.

"I got this, MaddyJo," he said with a smile and walked toward the flipping part of the counter. Raising it he said, "Come on back."

"Thank you," said Eilida, unsure about everything, but everyone appeared friendly. This place was an undiscovered part of her.

"Take a seat." He motioned her to sit in a fluffy leather chair with gold buttons on the side. The walls of the small office were covered in decades or more of Billows Hollow officers. A young Burkhalder stood out to her, standing beside a young blond man. Taking in his kind face one more time, she realized it was a young Jackson Martin.

He sat across from her and lifted his arms upwards, tenting his hands. "It's a pleasure to meet you. I was great friends with your parents. I'd known your father since grade school."

She brushed her sweaty palms against her jeans. "That's what Burkhalder said too. You were all friends?"

He smiled. "Some of the best memories of my life were with the two of them."

"Can you tell me about him?"

A twinkle caught his eye. "Your father was a hardworking man who loved people, especially his beautiful wife and family. Your mother, you look a lot like her…" he paused for a second, "caught his eye the moment he laid eyes on her."

For several minutes they discussed her parents and it eased her nerves. She didn't remember much about them, yet remembered the horror of Hurricane Chloe vividly.

"Do you mind telling me about the night… the hurricane?"

He nodded, and the twinkle in his eye receded, then he gave a heavy sigh. "Alice and I were checking out the island, makin' sure everyone was safe, or at the shelter. We knew the storm was comin' in but never expected Chloe to be so powerful. Alice called me, said she found a young girl trapped in her car in a ditch and to meet her at the hospital. I turned tail around and headed there straight away. We all knew this girl. Sweet thing, but dumber than a doorpost and the worst taste in men. At the hospital, Alice paced — nerves. She didn't believe the girl had ran off the road. Nope." He shook his head for emphasis.

"She believed there was foul play. Alice always had an eye for that. I stood by her. The doc bandaged her up best he could, then a young couple we didn't know appeared at the ER doors. She was in labor and the doc and nurse rushed her in. Later that night, while Alice and I were catchin' a wink a sleep, we heard the baby cry. And what a proud daddy. He picked up Alice and twirled her in the air before he realized what he was doin'. Settin' her down, we followed him into the room and caught a look at the sweet baby. Dillon was his name. I dunno whatever happened to him, but what a ray of sunshine."

He smiled, then continued. "It wasn't long after our smiles faded when we learnt the storm had been upgraded to a cat 4!" He raised his brows. "Our first thoughts were of your family. The roof and walls crackin' and the storm strengthenin', nothing we could do but get everyone in the ER to safety and that's just what we did. In the mornin' we headed to the beach and Alice found you in the arms of a young man we'd seen earlier the previous day headin' towards the beach. She directed him to the shelter but he never made it. Then he disappeared without a trace, but she always thought he was guilty and she was right. Never doubted that."

Hearing about her parents and baby Dillon gave her a smile, but thoughts of the monster holding her sent chills over her body in waves as she remembered him singing Delilah.

"Over the years I've stayed in contact with Alice and it wasn't until a few years ago they discovered how he escaped without bein' seen. He hitched a ride with a man headin' out of Billows Hollow and snatched his arrowhead. The same arrowhead was found at a crime scene in 2007 I believe. Fingerprints were all over it and they pulled the guy for questionin'. Turns out he hadn't seen the arrowhead for years." The words ran off his tongue with distaste.

He turned his eyes downward. "I'm really sorry."

Eilida fought back tears and cupped her nose in her hands to fight off the stinging. "You did what you could, under the circumstances. I'm glad she found me, and my aunt and uncle have always been wonderful parents to me. They love me like their own."

They both sat quiet for a couple minutes then, Eilida asked, "What happened to the girl trapped in her car?"

He smiled. "She survived and got married to a nice man a few years later. Still married, last I heard."

He shifted his eyes towards hers and lay his hand across the desk. She lifted her hand and placed it in his palm. "You and that baby were two shining lights in that storm."

She smiled as a tear escaped her eye.

He perked up and a wide smile crossed his handsome face. "A few years later, I married the nurse. We have twins. They're, uh, teens now but my wife's off today and a great cook. Why don't you join us for dinner and we can put you up for the night? It's dark and the weather isn't favorable for drivin'."

Eilida nodded and let go of a curl she'd been twirling in her fingers. She felt safe with this man. He was a part of her father, a man who was stolen from her at such a young age. "I'd like that."

Who's There?

From a distance, Tommy observed Eilida walk out of the small building marked *Billows Hollow Police* with a tall, thinish, good-looking man with dirty blond hair. She got into her car and he took the driver's seat of a police cruiser that said *Sheriff* on the side. They acted as though they knew each other and a hint of familiarity pinged in Tommy's head. He wondered if the man was friends with his parents before they moved.

Eilida followed the Sheriff's car and Tommy, out of curiosity, followed her, keeping distance between them. He wanted to know their connection and why she was in Billows Hollow. They drove a few blocks through town, then parked outside a single family home. It was a brick square with a porch on the front and a small window overlooking the porch. White hurricane shutters were propped open and evergreen shrubs were planted against the front porch.

He didn't pull onto the road, instead he parked in front of a house that appeared empty. In fact, more homes than not didn't have cars in the driveway, but it was a beach community and survived off spring through summer tourism. He slipped back in his seat. The car was so small his knees hit beneath the steering wheel. From his viewpoint, though, he observed them walk into the house.

Few lights came on in any of the houses, so he took that as them being empty and got out of his car. It served to stretch his legs that had been crunched behind the steering wheel of the tiny car, but also fed his curiosity. Rerolling his man bun, he pushed the black ball cap tight over his head and strolled down the street, sticking to the opposite side of the house Eilida entered with the Sheriff.

Inside the homes, lights flashed from people's TVs and others sat around tables passing dinner. In the cop's house, a large window gave him a clear picture of the family, plus Eilida, eating dinner. A smile on her face, she laughed and threw her hair over her shoulder, then took a bite. Two kids sat at the table, a boy and a girl. He figured them about fifteen, maybe sixteen. A woman, her back to the window, sat across from Eilida with the cop at the head of the table. No doubt this was the Sheriff's family, but how did Eilida fit into the picture?

Back at his car, he started the motor and drove to the nearest pharmacy in preparation for plan B.

Eilida snuggled onto an air mattress in the living room that Mrs. Martin had fixed for her. Her mind raced backwards as if stuck in a time warp. The entire family went to bed and she struggled to sleep, tossing and turning. Her parents had been the "nice" couple. *Was the town full of this type of people? People who let strangers inside their home?*

She was Jim and Lilly's daughter, but that didn't mean she wasn't crazy or psychopathic. She wasn't, and was thankful daily that craziness didn't reside in the traits of her family, but Sheriff Jackson Martin didn't know that. He didn't know her. The thought process brought her full circle to the stranger who her parents so willingly welcomed into their home. A man who forever changed the course of her life.

Darkness surrounded her, yet comfort existed inside. This man had, without question, let her into his home with his family. His most prized and loved in life. She closed her eyes to sleep and almost succumbed until a rattle outside made her shoot upward. The blanket covering her body slid off the couch. Against her better judgment, but knowing she was safe inside the four walls surrounding her, traipsed toward the window. She pushed the curtain to the side and peeked into the darkness. Nothing. Then a shadow caught her attention from the corner of her eye. Her head jerked toward the shadow, but emptiness existed. No shadow. *Was it her imagination?*

A crash sounded from upstairs. The twins. She jolted towards the steps, then heard the teens giggling at one another. She hadn't been upstairs, but Jackson Martin told her they shared the loft. When the twins were five, they divided off the room and made two rooms out of the large area. Taking a couple steps backwards, she turned on her heel and went back to the air mattress, put in her earbuds and pressed the music icon on her phone then scrolled through until she found the collection she wanted. Within a few undistracted minutes, she fell asleep.

Tommy set his alarm early. The compact car was far too small for him to sleep inside of, so he'd checked into a motel for the night and paid cash. Eyeing his pharmacy purchase, and being sure it was accessible, he tossed the bag onto the passenger seat and headed toward the Sheriff's house.

Her car still parked out front, he sighed relief that she hadn't left yet. It was another couple hours before she ventured to her car, the family seeing her out. *Isn't that sweet*, he thought.

With a thermos he imagined filled with hot, steaming coffee, she climbed into her car. He glanced at the cardboard cup beside him, the coffee long gone, and wished he was with her. The night before last she'd cried on his shoulder and slept on his lap. He woke up on cloud nine. Today, he shrugged as he watched her back from the spot her car was parked and pull onto the main road. *What did I do? What did I not do?* he questioned to the air.

He didn't have a clue where she was going. She wasn't following the same path. Staying several car lengths behind, he tailed her. When she turned onto US-64, Horn City came to mind. *But what business did she have in Horn City?* More than curious, he followed her off US-64 onto US-13 and into suburbia. Horn City.

She stopped outside an older home. It looked abandoned. The street wasn't deserted, just that house. She climbed out of her car and, one slow step at a time, walked towards the front door.

Eilida walked towards the house. She found it while researching. Evan O'Conner, the monster, was a victim of child abuse. It didn't make his crimes less important, but it gave her something. Under more favorable conditions, maybe he'd have used his energy for something more positive than destroying the lives of others. Shifting her eyes around the neighborhood she noted large trees and homes in need of minor repairs. Taking in a deep breath, she steadily walked towards the looming front door. It grew as she neared it. Finally, the large wooden frame stood directly in front of her.

She closed her eyes and turned the knob, never expecting it to be unlocked. A shiver ran down her spine when it opened. Hazy light filtered through the windows as she entered the dark lair. The monster, Evan O'Conner's, childhood home. She lifted her foot and took a brave step, then another, and walked into the home. It was empty, void of furniture and evidence of any crime. A layer of dust settled over the floor and curtains that still hung in the windows.

Her mind saw a dead Mr. O'Conner in a recliner by the large living room window, blood trailing to, and puddling on, the floor around him. Two small blond children ran past her, one a bubbly, curly headed Emily and the other the innocent younger brother of Evan. From the hall she heard a woman wail in pain. She knew it all existed within her mind, yet the wail made goose bumps crawl up her arms.

A curly blond-headed boy, no more than ten, took a lashing from a leather belt in front of her eyes. The swish of the Hyde broadcast across the room. She dropped to the ground and covered her face. Tears flowed like a river filled with melting snow. Trepidation and sadness settled within her soul. For the first time she saw the monster as a person, not a beast, and she shed tears for the horrific monster he became. She'd read about him when researching and couldn't completely understand until walking into the house of horrors. He was a boy that had been subjected to rejection and hate from the people who should love him most. They molded Evan O'Conner into a psychopathic serial killer. At the moment, she hated his parents more than she hated him.

A small creak caught her attention, but was so absorbed in the ghosts that inhabited the home of death she didn't know from which direction it came. Turning her head side to side, she examined the room, then slowly rose from the ground and sauntered towards the kitchen. Upon seeing it empty, she took a very deep breath before taking a couple steps backwards. Her neck pinched and she drew her hand towards the sharp pain, then the room spun and she dropped.

You're Safe With Me

Eilida woke on a large bed with a powder blue down comforter. It was soft beneath her body. Nothing was familiar. *Where am I?* she whispered. Drawing the comforter close to her chin, she glanced around the room. A small cherry nightstand was beside the bed and a large cherry dresser with a mirror stood across from her. On the nightstand was a couple pieces of toast and a glob of jelly, along with a bottled water. Not trusting the food, she tested the bottle. The cap hadn't been removed so she turned it and took a large swig of water.

Footsteps sounded and moved closer to the room. Eilida braced herself and dread welled inside her gut. She turned in the bed and dragged the cover up to her eyes, then squeezed them shut as the door knob twisted.

She listened. The footsteps were heavy, as if the person was tall but soft and gentle. When they walked past the bed she opened an eye then closed it as the footsteps drew closer to her face.

"Eilida," sounded a familiar voice. Her inner reaction was fear mixed with the same strange feeling of safety she'd always felt around him. She dared to pop her eyes open again.

Tommy knelt beside the bed Eilida slept in. Her brown waves covering her flawless face. He lifted them off her cheek and laid them over her shoulder, then ran a finger over her cheek. He knew she wasn't still asleep since he'd only given her a small dose and she'd obviously taken a drink from the bottle of water.

Her deep blue eyes stared at him, filled with fear, and she jolted upward, drawing her knees to her chest. "What the hell, you freak!"

He deserved that, but was still taken aback by her accusation. "How do you feel?"

She tilted her head. "I dunno. How should I feel?" Her eyes widened with the response.

His Adam's apple bobbed as he swallowed. Tommy didn't want to intimidate her, so stood and walked towards the long dresser with the mirror and leaned his butt against it, his fingers curled over the edge. "Confused, scared?"

"What the… How the hell did I get here and where is here?" The words tumbled from her mouth with fire.

"I found you and brought you here, my parents' home. You were unconscious." It wasn't a one hundred percent lie. He did find her and they were in his parents' home.

She wrinkled her face. "Thought your parents were dead?"

"They are. The house is now mine," he slipped his hands into his front pockets.

Her face lit up and she jumped out of bed, drawing the curtain beside it back. She peered out the window then turned around, her eyes narrowed. "You found me. Just casually found me. Ha! No way! Were you following me?"

He was glad he'd traded in the other rental car. It was always better to be safe than sorry. "Like I said, you were unconscious, and why all the hate towards me? I searched the address. That's the home he grew up in. Killed his family in." He wanted to know why the heck she would go to Evan O'Conner's childhood home. His crimes against his family so heinous that, to this day, the house stood empty.

She leaned against the window sill, across from where he stood. "Unfinished business," she jeered, "and it's none of yours." She finished the statement by folding her hands over her chest.

"Well someone didn't want you there, so it was lucky I found you." He brought his hands over his chest to challenge her face off.

She narrowed her eyes into slits. "The only way you'd know I was there was if you followed me. I think you've been stalking me for a while now. There's too many coincidences. You leave Sandy at my hospital bedside, then you turn up at my college, and suddenly you're rescuing me from the monster's home."

He turned his gaze from her to the floor, then back to her. She was right, but he wouldn't admit it to her. If he hadn't followed her, who knows what might have happened? His stay at Poppy Hills and his years hanging out with Scarlett taught him to lie. And the knockout serum he'd learned from Evan. Not directly, but he'd found one of his recipes. *Was he like Evan?*

Through all of this, he wanted nothing more than for Eilida to trust him, but why should she? She had no reason to believe him. He hadn't told her many truths. He lifted himself off the dresser and walked towards the door, saying nothing.

Damn him and that Moon, Pluto, and Saturn thing that fed his emotional need to take control and be overprotective, and helpful. Jeez, and Venus too. Yet his Moon, Venus, and Sun in Cancer gave him the qualities she adored.

Eilida twisted her mouth and scanned the room. *Where's my stuff? Where's my car?* Burying her face in her hands, she took a deep breath. A mixture of panic, sadness, and horror made her body shake. Taking more deep breaths, she calmed. She was wearing a large T-shirt – no doubt one of Tommy's.

She pulled herself together and walked out of the room, and followed the short hallway that emptied into a living room where Tommy sat on a gold leather sofa. He'd taken the band out of his hair and it spilled over his cheek. *He's so freakin' sexy!* She squeezed her eyes and pushed the thought to the back of her mind. His head turned as the hardwood floor creaked beneath her feet, and the pale blue in his eyes appeared gray and sad. *Damn if he doesn't look good enough to jump his bones.* She hated that she thought it.

"I need my stuff," she said in a notch above a whisper, after she wrapped her hands against the edge of the wall.

Tommy blew the hair from his face and nodded. After a couple minutes, he pushed off the couch and walked towards her. As he swept past her, he pulled his chest in and didn't look her in the eye. Wetness lingered in the corner of his eyes and a single tear dropped against his cheek.

He turned into a room and reappeared with her bag, which he dropped at her feet as he moved past her. If he was playing a guilt trip on her, it was working. He'd never actually done anything to harm her… yet she always found a way to turn every situation around. Biting her tongue, she walked back to the bedroom, bag in hand.

Was she that mean? Did he really save her? She remembered hearing something, then feeling a sharp sting in her neck. The Hurricane Killer used needles to deliver drugs to incapacitate his victims, making them putty in his hands. *Is Tommy his protégé and picking up where he left off?*

If she didn't know for sure the Hurricane killer, AKA Evan O'Conner, was dead, she'd think this was all part of one of his wicked plans to trap and kill her. Yet, she'd spent hours with Tommy and never once did he ever harm her. That fact continued to run rampant in her thoughts.

She pulled up her jeans that had more holes than a sponge and slipped off his T-shirt, replacing it with her hoodie, then wiggled her feet into her shoes.

Checking her phone, the battery was nearly dead, so she plugged it in. It would be a couple hours before it was fully charged. Before turning it off she checked her GPS: *she was in South Carolina? Why bring her all the way here and not to his home in North Carolina?* It was much closer. It didn't make sense. The Tommy she'd come to know seldom made logical decisions. *Emotionally driven, rationalizing his emotions, that what his chart reads and, boy, it fits him. Was she being too hard?*

Tommy still sat on the couch and she needed her car. She slid onto a chair kitty corner to him. "Where's my car?"

He shifted his eyes toward her and clasped his hands. "It's where you left it."

She nodded. "Why did you bring me here?"

"It was the safest place I could think of. Somebody is trying to harm you. Who would know you were there? No one, unless they were tailing you. Who broke into your apartment? Somebody is trying to scare you." He sighed and his chest heaved up and down.

Protector Tommy. She considered his words, and he had a point. Someone had tried to strike fear into her and it had worked. Reluctantly, she apologized, but wasn't fully convinced of anything yet. She erred on the side of caution. Squirrely Neptune, the planet of deception, she had yet to meet the real Tommy.

His eyes soft, he said, "I want you safe. If you prefer, I'll take you back to your car or take you home. I'll even sit outside your apartment to be sure no one breaks in."

She twisted her mouth then replied, "Tomorrow, we'll do it then. Right now I'm hungry and could use a beer."

He perked up. "I don't have a Heineken, but I'm sure there's something alcoholic in the fridge." He stood and walked to the kitchen, his pants hanging just right on his round ass-cheeks. *Damn, why did she want him so bad?* She'd lost Jay, maybe not, they had agreed to a break, and all she could do was check out Tommy, the possible psychopath.

Several minutes later, he returned with a Bud Light and a sandwich. He handed her the plate, a napkin, then the beer, and sat beside her, taking her free hand between his.

"I've never felt about anyone the way I feel about you. I know you don't trust me, but I'll never hurt you." He let go of her hand and ran the tips of his fingers across her cheeks. Everything inside her tingled and wetness soaked her panties. She wanted him more than the food or the beer. She needed him inside her. She placed her beer on the floor and caught the hand against her cheek in hers. Leaning towards him, she yearned for his lips on hers and, when they met, another burst of wetness soaked through her jeans which she wanted to rip off. He leaned closer to her and sunk his hands beneath her ass, cupping it, then pulled her upwards onto him. His fingers moving at lightning speed, he unbuttoned her jeans and slipped his hands into her pants.

"You're so wet," he whispered as his mouth brushed against her ear.

"I feel your hard cock through my jeans. You are so huge," she moaned.

"I want you," he said as he stood, lifting her to her feet and pulling down her pants. She hurriedly pulled down his and stopped to actually take a look at his manhood. It was huge, even larger than it felt.

He pulled her towards him and they rubbed against each other as their mouths met. Her hands rubbing against the piece of him she yearned for. He wrapped his arms around her, smashing her against him. He throbbed against her and she knew how much he wanted her. Eilida jumped and wrapped her legs around him. He caught her and pulled her warm, wet pussy just above his throbbing cock.

No doubt he was teasing her. His tip met her clit and he moved her ass, wiggling her against it, but not maneuvering himself inside. She couldn't take it, wetness soaked against him and dribbled down the sides of his cock. She pushed against him, wanting so much to feel him inside her. He lifted her up, keeping her from thrusting and engulfing him.

"Tommy," she moaned. "I'm about to cum. Oh... I need you now!" Her voice raised an octave as he slid her onto him. She wasn't kidding. As soon as he pushed inside her she erupted in an orgasm. His cock was so wet between her and his pre-cum, he slid right in and it felt too good. Riding with her orgasm, she wrapped her arms around his neck and used it as leverage to propel herself and thrust her hips against him.

He walked to the back of the couch and leaned her over it, her dark hair spilling onto the cushions beneath her. He thrust into her hard. His dick growing larger, driving her to the edge of ecstasy. Then wet heat sprayed inside her as they moaned in pleasure. Their releases meeting each other's.

They continued making love long into the evening, a fire crackling and their shadows moving in rhythm together. After a few hot and sweaty hours, they rested against one another. He lifted and propped his head onto his hand. "Shower time?" he said, more as a question.

"Go ahead," she responded, stretching her arms over her head.

He nodded and Eilida watched him pick up his clothes and head down the hall, naked, admiring the round curve of his ass. The sound of running water resonated through the hallway. She scooted upwards and sat upright, then exhaled as she rose and padded toward the bedroom. Instead of the one that held her clothes, she went into the room he'd walked into earlier. She assumed it was his room. Tommy's head peeked around the doorframe.

"The water's hot. Join me." He licked his lips and then he was gone.

He had an open duffle bag that sat near the bed. The chain of her pendant was tangled in the back of her hair. Leaning her head down, she worked to untangle the chain. After struggling for a few seconds, and cringing as she pulled it from the knots surrounding it, the pendant dropped. Her eyes darted around the floor searching, but didn't see it. Something shiny twinkled from his bag. She reached in and it sank further. Her hands, chasing the pendant, dug deep into the bag. A solid object at the bottom of the bag got her attention. As she lifted it out her eyes grew wide and she dropped it. A hunting knife in a leather sheath lay on the ground beside her.

Taking a few deep breaths to calm herself, she picked it up. Why does he have a knife? Worst case scenario, and the one presently repeating inside her mind, was he planned to use it on her and finish what the Hurricane Killer didn't.

"Eilida."

She jumped at the sound of her name and decided in that second to stash it under the dresser.

"Be right there, looking for something to wear." She slid it far enough under the dresser he wouldn't be able to see it, then grabbed jeans and a sweatshirt and laid them on the bed.

Tommy stuffed the last bite of the largest burger she'd ever seen into his mouth. Eilida sat across from him, took a swig of beer and nibbled at her burger.

"My parents used to bring me here all the time when I was a kid." He lifted his beer and took a gulp, placing it back on the wooden table.

She forced a smile and nodded as she chewed her food. Her eyes focused on a rustic fish painting behind Tommy. He tilted his head to meet her gaze but she'd shift her eyes away from his.

"Are you OK?" he asked, her tension that obvious.

She blinked, then finally met his eyes for a brief second. "Yeah, I guess I'm zoning out from all that driving."

His instincts didn't buy it. Something was amiss and he'd have to work to figure it out, or piss her off. He had no plans to piss her off and wished she'd just trust him.

She perked up. "Soo," she twisted her lips, "this hamburger was amazing, but I'm stuffed."

He grabbed a fry off her plate, observing her half-eaten bacon Swiss burger and motioned for the waitress.

"I'm going to visit the little girls' room." She scooted off the seat and scurried to the bathroom.

She went straight to a stall, closed the door, and yanked her cell out of her pocket. She clutched her pendant. *Why don't I get weird vibes from him? Damnit, he carries a knife sheathed in leather.* Instead of fear she felt safe, protected by him. His soft blue eyes sent warmth and concern and his actions were about protection.

Was the knife for protection?

She thought to call Sage, her bestie, but didn't want her driving all the way from Chesterville. She thought of Burkhalder, who lived in South Carolina, but she was recovering from a car wreck.

Jay was rightfully upset with her. No way could she call her overprotective aunt-and-uncle-parents. They'd freak out and worry about the danger. She was on her own to get herself out of the current pickle.

Always a Back Up Plan

Tommy walked to the wall and wrapped his hands around a gold filigree, eleven by seven picture frame. Inside was a picture of a little blond boy playing on the beach. He lifted it off the wall and set it upright against a table. A metal door to a wall safe was behind it. After rotating the combination, the lock clicked and he opened it up. Inside was a solid screen and a touch keypad. He pressed his thumb against the screen and typed in a code. It popped open, revealing a stack of papers.

He pulled them out and carried them to the glass-surfaced modern dining room table and spread them out. Eilida strolled up behind him and peered around him. She knew what and whose they were. A cold breeze swept past her, sending a flutter of chills over her body, and a lump settled in her stomach.

He shifted his gaze to her. "Are you ready?"

She sucked in a deep breath to calm her body. "I'll never be ready, but since the accident I set a goal to face my fears." She took a step from behind him and another couple towards the table. A mass of astrological charts – back-ups – and a tablet laid out before her. Eilida gulped as Tommy flipped through each chart.

"He had all these, too? That means they were all possibilities…" her voice trailed off.

"There's more," he said, opening the tablet. Eilida read over Evan's handwritten scribbles and wasn't surprised that his writing was very neat.

Life number 4
Mars retrograde every two years
The midpoint is 3

Tommy grabbed his phone off the table and opened a Google search. After a few minutes he spoke. "A life number of four is someone who tends towards organization, methodical planning, and deep commitment."

He was all of those things, she thought. She plucked the phone out of his hands, went to Patrice's website and searched on Mars Retrograde. Her breath caught and she took steady breaths to keep from hyperventilating. "Mars retrograde is a bad time to start something new, but there's something else that may be of interest," she stated with an unsteady voice.

"Yeah…"

"Mars rules metals and action, so anything made from it may not work as expected…" Her words hung in the air like thick ground fog. "He used… a… metal." Her mouth formed an O.

He nodded, deep in thought. *Midpoint*, was he talking astrology? Tommy studied it again. Repeating the term *midpoint* in his mind. Then he got it. "By choosing the midpoint or the middle – median – number he'd avoid his *tools*," he wasn't sure the proper word to use, but tools sounded better than knives, "malfunctioning or rather him malfunctioning while using them."

The hair on her body stood on end. "That's one way of putting it."

He took a seat beside her as he absorbed everything. "It also said Mars retrograde isn't an exact two years apart, plus using the three year intervals, eventually it would catch up to him."

Her brain spinning like a hamster on a wheel, an idea clicked. Tommy was born after a solar eclipse which meant the moon was in the new moon phase. Astrology was a big part of the story, but lunar phases had meanings too. She pulled her phone out of her pocket as she asked, "Do you have scratch paper around here?"

He shifted, then walked to a small table with a drawer underneath. He opened the door and pulled out a pen and notepad, handing it to her.

She pulled out a seat, and opened the moon phase app on her phone. Plugging in the dates, she scribbled the results on the paper.

He eyed her but didn't speak.

She laid the pen on the table. "You were born after a solar eclipse, meaning the moon was in line with the Earth and Sun. It was a new moon. A time for new beginnings. You were born that night during a wicked hurricane and, by all accounts, shouldn't have lived, but you're here." She cleared her throat and did her best to keep an analytical mind so she wouldn't get emotionally gobbed up. "Evan performed his first ritual serial killing that night. His family doesn't count. That was driven by his emotion as a Cancer and not by astrology per se. He was a child and not yet a follower of astrology, so wouldn't have known or understood the interpretation of a chart. We have two new beginnings that night, tied to this one event."

He slid his hands into his back pocket. "You're saying that we need to study each moon phase?"

"No, well, kind of. We need to get our transit charts for that night," she replied with enthusiasm. Without hesitation she picked up her phone and dialed Patrice.

Breaking Free

Eilida talked with Patrice and couldn't do anything more until she had a chance to get the charts finished. Her plan now was to not let on that she'd found the knife and to get the hell out of his house without him attempting to stop her.

She pulled off her hoodie and headed toward the hallway. "Changing into sweats," she called as she disappeared around the corner. Tommy dropped his keys on the table by the door, then went directly to the fire to turn the coals and add more wood.

Eilida reappeared in sweats. "What kind of movies do you have?" she asked as she sat sideways on the couch.

Tommy smiled. "Not many, but we can make a few," he responded, lifting an eyebrow.

She punched him in the shoulder. "Or not."

"Ouch," he teased, rubbing the spot she'd hit him. "The movies are over there," he said, pointing to a wooden cabinet.

Opening the doors, she sifted through the movies. "Who likes all the chick flicks?"

"My mom," he responded, a touch of melancholy in his voice. His mother's favorite was The Notebook with Rachel McAdams. He didn't care for the movie, but had a huge crush on her when he was younger. Eilida tilted her head and twirled a strand of hair as she sifted through the movies.

"I got it!" she turned and ran-jumped onto the couch beside Tommy. He bounced from her impact with the couch. In her hand was *Die Hard*.

The rain beat against the house and Eilida snuggled against Tommy and fell asleep half way through the movie. Her head leaned against his shoulder, he smoothed her hair. He and his dad watched this movie a hundred times. A day never went by when he didn't feel the pain their deaths caused.

A crackle of lightning burst through the sky, lighting the entire room, taking him back to Scarlett. Every time it rained he thought of their talks.

"I never had a home. The daughter of a rapist is a lonely life. Kids at school had parents and siblings. I bounced from foster home to foster home and wasn't at any school long enough to make friends, but I did feel the wrath of their

bullying. The day I met my sister, my own blood sister, I was so happy. We looked so much alike, there was no doubt. Here she was, married to a wealthy man. They offered for me to stay with them. I was like Cinderella at the ball."

A creeping blackness covered her eyes as she continued. "That happiness only lasted a short time. They were sex freaks and wanted me for him, for her wrinkly, old husband so she could watch. Do you believe that, my own sister?!"

Pain radiated off her and an eerie darkness shadowed the room. He didn't know what to say, and couldn't imagine how she felt.

She clasped her hands and bared her teeth. "I was a virgin and refused, so they drugged me and he… raped me." Tears rolled across her cheeks as the words dropped from her mouth. "He got me pregnant and they held me there against my will. I tried to self-abort the baby. I didn't want a baby born of rape, like me. I know what that life is like." She sobbed.

Tommy jumped from his seat and brought her a box a tissues. Tenderly, he dabbed at her tears, still unsure what to say.

"Nine months later," she sniffled, "Evan O'Conner was born."

Tommy's eyes widened with the revelation. She told him all about the evil inside Evan, but now she was saying that she was his mother.

She looked him in the eye, her gaze diving into his soul. "They were so happy with the little monster, I escaped. Never did I return, but I kept tabs on them. When his father died from a heart attack, I thought it was a higher power giving me justice. But years later, when he murdered his mother, I laughed. She got what she sowed in life. Karma isn't only a bitch. She's a supreme bitch."

Tommy gulped and blew a few stray hairs out of his face. "You're his mother," he stammered.

She nodded, and the sadness in her face dissipated as she smiled. "But if I could choose, I'd have a son just like you." She cupped his chin in her hand. "You're sweet, gentle, caring. The days you visit, my life feels complete. We're kindred family. Maybe not blood, but by a higher power."

Eilida trembled next to him. He wound his arm tight around her, then lifted beneath her legs with the other and carried her to the bed.

Tommy carrying her to bed woke her up, but she pretended to still sleep. She listened to his breathing as he snuggled beside her and, when his breaths became shallow, she climbed out of bed, grabbed the bag she'd packed earlier when she changed into sweats. She'd watched where he placed the keys and grabbed them up, then turned the lock on the door as quietly as she could.

She didn't want to wake him. Peeling the door open, she looked into the rain, quivered, then shut the door behind her, careful it didn't close hard. Waking Tommy was the last thing she wanted. Scurrying through the rain, her heart thumping against her chest like a drummer, she unlocked his car door and slid into the driver's seat. The little car started and purred so quiet she almost couldn't tell it was running.

After she backed from the driveway with the lights off so they wouldn't shine against the house she flipped them on and sped off through the night.

A draft of cold air hit Tommy's face, that had been buried in Eilida's hair. Patting the bed beside him, he realized she wasn't there. His heart pounded inside his chest and he leaped out of bed and rushed to the window.

"Damnit, Eilida!" he screamed. Every time he thought he had her, she escaped. Tonight was one of the best of his life. The two of them, snuggled by a fire watching a movie, carrying her to bed after hours of sex. He wanted her so bad, he tried to convince her she was in trouble.

Astrology Does it Again!

Eilida did her best to push any memories of Tommy into a dusty corner of her mind. He was bad news and Patrice confirmed it. Well, not Patrice, but the charts. They didn't say he was the guilty party but they sure did point in that direction. But they also suggested someone else was a possibility.

May 8, 2014, was an anomaly and played out well by each person involved, as if they were puppets. Eilida sat with hers and Tommy's transit charts from Patrice, plus she had Evan's copy of his own. He wrote:

Midheaven opposes my ascendant at 29 Scorpio, I take a personal hit. Uranus in the 8th opposed by Mars = unexpected violent death – Emily and family, me too? Mercury in the 10th press coverage and public knowledge. Sun in 9th rules 12th of hidden enemies, opposite Saturn = involvement of authority figure – Carrot Top Cop? Sun Trine to Pluto, a mystery solved, whose? Pluto in 5th house, by one of the kids?

No, my destiny is not tied into this chart. You will not dictate my actions! I have free will!

Yeah, no doubt the monster had several marbles loose. A complete narcissistic asshole, she thought. He interpreted his own chart and didn't bother to heed its warning. Clear and plain it warned of his death. What gave her more chills was the mystery solved part – her mystery. She was the kid! And poor Erica. Her heart dropped, thinking of the little girl who lost her family. The mystery of The Hurricane Killer. It most definitely had media coverage, which she planned to renew with her own term paper. A memory hit her smack in the folds of her holey brain. In Chesterville, she wrote a Dear Delilah column for the local paper and, just previous to May 8th, she received a letter.

She clicked around a bit on her computer then pulled up her old Dear Delilah stuff. Like a packrat, she'd saved her advice. A man named Ted wrote her a letter about his sister, and she responded with sound advice. On May 8th he responded. She didn't see his response until much later, but his email said:

Dear Delilah,

This is Ted again. I want to thank you for your advice. I have been in touch with my sister. In fact, I will be meeting her and her family tonight. Thank you, Ted.

Undeniably, it was him. *Was it a warning? Or was it his inflated ego?* It didn't matter, the monster dug a ditch deep into her soul. The more she thought about it the more she realized it was his way of flipping a metaphorical bird at his transit chart.

Patrice designed a transit chart for Evan that said pretty much the same thing his did. She had to admit, he was good. She'd looked over all his charts and discussed them with Patrice and he was dead on each one. The man used them to decide which days to kill and karma boomeranged, but with his inflated ego he completely ignored the warning. No — challenged the warning on purpose as if he was an indestructible god whose free will could change the outcome.

He'd noted the opposition to his Scorpio ascendant, which represented him, from the Midheaven of the event chart as a personal hit, yet ignored how deadly it really was. Scorpio ruled death and its last degree, the 29th, further implied a permanent ending. Certainly, that had been the story of his life, which he'd imposed on far too many people. The event chart's Midheaven opposing his ascendant implied his status at that moment could represent an ending. He may have seen that as him taking someone else's life, except coming from the 7th house of relationships implied someone he knew would be involved, not a random victim. With a start, she remembered that the 7th included open enemies. Someone who openly hated him, whereas hidden enemies, who resided in the 12th house, were more elusive.

Eilida did the research and identified the lunar phases for each of the monster's slaughters. It was fascinating that they began with the New Moon/Solar Eclipse, then progressed through the phases. The two following were waxing crescents, then the next two were waning gibbous, the last one, waning crescent, ready to start a new cycle. In looking at each of the event charts, it was also hard to ignore that, every time he killed, there were heavy transits to his natal 8th house of death, four of the six triggering his deadly Pluto, Moon, Mars, Sun pattern and the others hitting the Vertex, an energy point that typically involves fate, placed in his 8th. Even if he hadn't been into astrology, he probably would have killed at those times as the cosmic energies activated his evil nature.

His death was a waxing gibbous moon. A time for cycles to culminate, then wind down toward new beginnings. Adding that to his transit chart, no doubt his life had ended and his killing spree was done. She didn't mind one bit that he challenged the chart because, if he hadn't, he'd still be killing and she wouldn't have her memories, although many of them were horror-filled, she also remembered her parents and brothers.

There was plenty more that Patrice found in the transit chart that targeted his death, and Tommy's chart pointed at him being involved with the monster's death. The sign of death and permanent endings along with indications for a new beginning.

The event chart's Sun ruling the ominous 12th house which included hidden enemies opposed Saturn that day, with Saturn relating not only to authority figures but also to responsibility and karma. Saturn was in Scorpio, the sign of death, *so death as a result of karma*. Mars was retrograde and it pointed at him doing something he'd later regret. She pondered how he'd chosen three year killing intervals. Mars retrograde wasn't an exact two years, after enough time it caught up to him and his own metal tool was turned against him. He definitely should have been careful with knives.

Jupiter in the event chart's 11th house showed a friendship was involved with the trine to Saturn indicating a friend facilitating a karmic deed or taking responsibility. Jupiter opposing Pluto implied taking control of a situation for a friend. Tommy knew the monster. She didn't know how close they were, because she'd avoided it. The thought gave her chills and an eerie feeling, but eying the chart and based on Patrice's words, maybe she should have given Tommy a chance to explain himself. If only he'd been honest with her, she might have done that. She sighed. Inside she really adored him.

One of the final curious aspects of the event chart was the Sun in sextile to Jupiter, providing an opportunity for a friend to express his opinion, with the Sun representing the 12th of hidden enemies. The trine between the Sun and Pluto showed a hidden enemy taking control. *Who was the monster's hidden enemy?* Tommy or, her gut said, it was someone else.

She already knew Tommy, and he'd returned Sandy. He took responsibility, as he'd done so many times since. *But who is the friend taking control?* Another aspect in each of their charts indicated Tommy was rebellious, whereas Evan's showed him being deceived, though it was possible that Evan had done it to himself by ignoring what the chart implied for the outcome.

Or maybe it was the ring. Tommy no doubt stole it, betraying and deceiving the monster. It was an Attractor and Tommy knew this. She and Sage told him. He stole it on purpose to send negative energy Evan's way. This made her believe in Tommy's innocence.

Now the real blow-your-mind information she collected was the extra work Patrice did, crossing her and Tommy's charts. They contained "love asteroids" such as Cupido. Tommy's conjuncted Eilida's ascendant, so love at first sight was the result. The asteroid Amor is pure and simple love and affection. Another bulls-eye. They have it in the same degree of Taurus, even though they were born in different years. All that, according to Patrice, adds up to a friendship developing between them no matter what.

Eilida didn't stop with comparing their charts on May 8, 2014. Since she'd never found a transit chart for Evan on June 30, 1992, she assumed his slaughter of her family that day wasn't planned with the correlation of astrology; for him it was a lucky hit. Or maybe he wasn't into astrology yet. It was also a solar eclipse which meant it was a new moon – a time for new beginnings. She shuddered at the thought.

Patrice had come through and the results made Eilida's skin crawl. Her chart showed a definite and sudden change in her home environment; a crisis involving her mother. Patrice's words, 'Uranus and Neptune in your 4th house of your natal chart are part of something known as the "natal promise" that your home life will experience sudden, disruptive events related to water.' It stung her heart even though the nightmare happened so long ago.

Her chart went as far as to indicate by Saturn's squaring of Pluto that she'd lose her father as well. Deception and hidden enemies were also clearly depicted. Everything that happened that day was written into the chart and her belief of astrology grew stronger the more she knew. It even indicated she'd never completely heal from the scars left that day.

Tommy's chart was no different. He had transiting planets that indicated the storm, deaths, and injuries. What she found particularly interesting about injuries was they were towards people in their homes. Her family was in their home and they invited in the monster. It indicated a sudden act of violence as well as the storm.

Evan's chart pushed a dagger deep into her heart as she'd listened to the details of it. His energy contained within the emotional sign of Cancer built up to explosive proportions. *And fucking Jupiter*, she thought, *ruler of his 4th house of home and environment which contained a strong Mars linked up with his Aries Moon, only increased his violence and thoughts towards his family.* That was only one nail in the coffin. The storm was there and his evil mother as well as the public's reaction to his blood fest. A shiver ran up her spine.

In the event chart when her parents were killed, the part where Eilida came in was transiting Pluto, ruler of death aspecting Evan's natal Chiron, an asteroid known as the "wounded healer," in his 5th house, indicating injury or death to a child, since the 5th house included children. The injury wasn't simply her, but both her brothers. And, ironically, it was part of his natal promise that he had been horribly injured as a child himself by his sick parents.

Each of their charts and events were set off by transiting planets and further exacerbated by the eclipse, an event that the ancients saw as an unfortunate omen. Shaking off the virtual bugs crawling on her skin, she thought of Tommy. He wasn't the guilty party, nor was he any danger to her. She wrapped a hand around her pendant, absorbing its energy, and picked up her phone with the other.

Cancer Aries Matchup

A week later and he still hadn't heard from Eilida. He'd made the choice to leave her be if that's what she really wanted. It ate him up inside, but nothing he tried convinced her he wasn't the bad guy and wasn't going to hurt her.

When he packed his belongings to leave his parents' house is when he realized his knife was missing and he assumed she found it. He didn't know how, but after two hours of searching the house he found it wedged beneath the dresser in his room. She drove him nuts! She discovered it and presumed he was going to use it on her or was the enemy. Either way, he had to practice patience. He could do that. After spending four years living with Evan, he'd learned patience.

All her astrology talk made him think. They'd only had brief conversations about their birthdays, mostly his. He didn't know which day she was born, only that she was an Aries. With that knowledge, he did his own research and learned he and Eilida were a typical Cancer/Aries matchup.

Unbelievable sex but lacking in communication. She was far too much of a wild card, while he was organized, efficient, and patient, and both of them displayed their emotions inappropriately in the other's eyes.

Every website said the same thing with different wording, convincing him. Reading and understanding made it easier for him to accept her strange behavior and even look at it from her point of view. They were fire and water and needed to feel in charge of various aspects of their lives. As he read, his emotions changed from dismayed to hopeful.

He spied her leaving the college library. She'd gone back to her pre-Tommy routine. Sadness settled inside him, watching how easy it appeared for her to push him aside.

Making the full circle of the parking lot, he eased back onto the main road and went to *Flashers*. The music and bustle of college students reminded him of the day he finally built up the nerve to talk with her and how he'd saved her from the punks on the trail.

His phone buzzed inside his pocket, interrupting his memory. A rope knotted in his belly as he pulled out his phone, expecting it to be Scarlett. His eyes widened and a smile stretched across his face when he saw Eilida's number.

He swiped the screen to answer. "Eilida."

Her breath was the first thing he heard as she released a sigh. "Tommy. I... um..." He listened as she stumbled over her words. "I've finished my research and, well, I need to show you everything."

He looked over his shoulder towards her apartment, then back to her car where, moments earlier, he'd planted the GPS tracker. "The charts?"

"Yes, but you have to be honest with me. I want to know the whole truth," she said in a demanding tone like his mother had used when assigning him chores.

He swallowed hard. "Where and when?"

"Now, at my apartment, while it's fresh in my mind."

Dirty thoughts of her naked filled his head. He'd do anything she asked and hoped there'd be a reconciliation that lasted. The whole truth would be hard, but he needed to do it. "Give me a few minutes."

He lied again, if only by admission but didn't want her to know he was stalking her — that'd freak her out

all over again. Tommy finished his beer,
then went to Eilida's.

Reconciliation

Tommy was more than confused when he knocked on Eilida's door. He didn't know whether she'd kick him out again, and out of her life completely and forever, or if she'd understand his story. She wanted the truth and he was going to give it to her no matter her reaction. He reminded himself of this as he knocked on her door.

It swung open and she stood before him in sweats that hung loose on her waist and a T-shirt with no bra beneath. Her nipples perked as the cold air rushed at them. She wore her long raven waves tied up in a sort of ponytail in which the ends stuck out from the top of her head. Unable to control himself, he smiled at the sight.

"Get in here, it's cold," she said, bringing her arms across her chest and rubbing her triceps for warmth.

One minute she was his friend, the next her enemy. No doubt she would always befuddle him. He stepped into her apartment and slid his jacket off as she closed and locked the door behind him.

Once the door was shut, she passed behind him and went straight to the refrigerator.

"Want a beer?" she asked, grabbing two Heinekens. It didn't matter his response; she was getting him a beer either way.

"Thanks," he responded, taking the cold beverage from her.

She backed up a couple steps and leaned against the bar. "I owe you an apology. I found your knife by accident. My pendant fell into your bag and when I reached in that huge chunk of metal came out. After losing time and waking up in your house, my mind thought all types of horrible thoughts. I've looked over all our transit charts, including the monster's and understand you have only been trying to protect me."

You're only realizing that now, after everything I've done to keep you safe? he thought. Tommy hadn't said a word. She'd dominated the conversation, leaving no room for him to respond in any way. He wasn't changing that now.

"The charts also let on that you knew the monster far better than you ever explained to me. I need the entire story, no matter how you think it'll affect me, I need it straight." Her dark eyes gave him a death glare.

He nodded and blew out a large breath, than twisted the shark's tooth around his neck. *I need strength, Mom.* Tuning his mind to the beginning. The day he walked in on Evan. He gave Eilida the full story this time, including the gory details. He relived the horror of his parents' death – the incident that led to his walking in on Evan. In his mourning, it was his best friend he reached out towards. When he walked into the house and heard the sounds, eerie sounds, he moved towards them and beaned Evan on the head hard enough to drop him unconscious. Scared and confused he ran smack into Scarlett.

The woman who became a surrogate mom. With Eilida's help, she forced him to see Scarlett as no better than Evan. She played on his emotional vulnerability. He sucked back the anger billowing inside for allowing her to misguide him. They planned, and everything went their way. Small tinges of sorrow, coupled with the anger, made it difficult for him to control his emotions and maintain his poker face.

He told her all about their plan to get rid of Evan. Tommy knew Evan was planning something big, as he'd been the one to deliver packages to the Turnwells at their old residence. The fact that he didn't know what was in the packages, or that Emily Turnwell was the woman Evan thought was his biological sister, didn't matter. He went along with Evan's plan and the guilt worked its way into Tommy's soul, devouring it.

He slowed his pace and met Eilida's disapproving gaze. The next part of the story was the toughest. It was the part he didn't want to say. He didn't want to relive it, but she wanted and deserved honesty. It would vindicate him and rip her apart. "Evan didn't only terrify the Turnwells into moving to the home he'd bought in Chesterville, but he set you up to live across the street. He never told me this, but I figured it out. He wanted you to feel the fear. Evan was more than a serial killer. He preyed on psychological games." Deep breaths, take a deep breath. "Evan murdered your grandmother in order to send you a message and make you relive the horror." He said it, and tears welled in Eilida's eyes. That part she hadn't expected.

Between choking sobs, she said, "No… not her," then folded her hands over her face and wept into them.

Tommy's instinct was to wrap his arms around her and allow Eilida to cry it out, but he wasn't sure if she'd bury her perfect face into his chest or push him

out the door. He teetered on the thought
a few seconds then couldn't take it
anymore and walked towards her,
enveloping her tiny frame in his solid
arms. She didn't protest as her body
trembled against him.

After a couple minutes, she lifted
her head; deep, water-filled sapphire eyes
stared at him. "Continue please," she
sniffled.

She wants more? He'd thought
that was all she could take, but she
wanted it all. This made him long for her
even more. Holding her close, he
persisted with the truth and explained
how he and Scarlett set up Evan. He
knew Evan was planning a getaway for
the two of them after he finished a
pharmaceutical "job." Tommy knew
better; that his job was anything but
selling legal drugs. He did as Evan
requested to keep himself in the clear so
he would be able to seduce him, plug him
in the neck with Evan's own needle and
drugs, then slit his neck and let him bleed
out the same as he did to all his victims.
It was a fitting end for such an
abominable man.

Scarlett's job was to watch Eilida
and meet him in Salvation Cove after
he'd killed Evan. They both knew Eilida
was involved in Evan's plan, they just

didn't exactly know how she fit into it. When Eilida slunk across the street and found the Turnwells' lifeless, bloody bodies, she hauled ass in the rain, slipping on the wet earth and tumbled to what Scarlett thought was her death. She told Tommy how she tried to catch her as she tripped on a root, but couldn't without tumbling the mountain with her. So she grabbed her keys and called 911.

Eilida gazed upwards at Tommy, her forehead scrunched in confusion. "She was the mysterious caller?"

He nodded.

"The monster was never in my car?"

He nodded again then responded, "No. Scarlett planted a pubic hair that I hijacked from his shower. I'd found all his charts and souvenirs. It freaked me out so bad, I nearly ran out of his room, then I gained my composure and thought. I needed DNA and I saw it."

She let out a huge sigh.

"I don't remember anyone on that mountain with me, but all my eyes saw were flashes between the Turnwells and my family and blood splattered everywhere. All my nightmares came back to me in one rush, then I hit the rock and nothing. In my mind you weren't you and I wasn't me. Nobody was themselves and my mother showed herself and each day brought me one step closer to remembering Hurricane Chloe," she said, drying up her sniffles.

"I'm sorry for everything," Tommy said, his voice gloomy and confused. She'd focused on Evan not actually being in her car, but the rest slipped past her. He didn't persist.

"No, this wasn't your fault. It was the monster's fault." She had to ask the question, even though in her heart she knew he didn't do it. "Did you kill him?"

"No," he said shaking his head. "I couldn't. I drugged him and brought the knife to his neck but… It got caught on the chain that he wore around his neck, sliced right through it, and both the chain and the ring on it fell onto the bed. In that moment I knew I couldn't kill him. If it hadn't caught I'd have gone through with the act and agonized the rest of my life over taking another."

She took a couple steps back from him, her hands on his waist. "So you did steal the ring?"

"Yeah, after you explained what it was used for I thought it couldn't hurt to send a little karma his way." He half-smiled.

She twisted her lips. "So who did it? Scarlett?"

"I don't know, but I don't think Scarlett had time to do it. She hated him, hated his father, but she's not a killer and I ran straight from the cabin to the car. She was inside it waiting. If she did it, I lost time somewhere."

She chuckled. "It's not funny, but it is. I have huge chunks of time missing from my mind."

His lips curved into a smile. "I never meant to deceive you. I wanted for so long to tell you everything, but the other part of me wanted only to keep you safe from harm and…" he twisted his lips, "and make you mine."

"Tommy, I care very much for you." She gave him a reassuring smile.

"I looked up Aries and Cancer matches online. I wasn't surprised. It said we have great sex but that's as far as our compatibility goes." His voice went from optimistic to sad in seconds.

She pulled him towards her, stood on her tiptoes and whispered in his ear, "I've looked at our charts and we have connections with the "love asteroids." We can't deny each other and will always have a strong connection."

He smiled, bringing his hands to her face. He cupped her chin and brought her mouth to his. "Is that right?" he said, his lips brushing against hers.

"Yes," she responded. He slipped his tongue inside her mouth and they kissed.

She was his and he wanted nothing more than to strip her bare and take her.

She pulled away. Her breath heavy. "I discovered so much more."

He lifted an eyebrow. "More?"

"You said July 7th, 2007. On that day, his lunar return chart hinted that somebody new would enter his life as something old departed. He met you even though he didn't know it and stopped his Hurricane Kills. Freaky, but every chart is an exact match to what happened." Her body gave an involuntary tremble beneath his fingertips.

It creeped him out, but didn't surprise him. Two years ago, he would have thought it bullshit, but not anymore. At the moment he was more concerned about the "love asteroids" and having his girl.

She traced his chest with a finger and he knew she felt his hardness pressing against her. "We are meant to be something and I care deeply for you. Most of the time I can't get you out of my mind, but my heart belongs to someone else if he'll still have me."

Tommy didn't care, he wanted her whether it meant sharing or not. He pulled her closer to him.

"I was wrong not to tell you about Jay. I need the balance of both of you in my life. You are as intense as me and seek powerful situations. You also bring a level of brute power and safety into my life. Jay is a sweetheart who has only ever wanted to please me and he fits like my favorite pair of jeans."

Her words penetrated inside him. *What is she saying?* he thought, wrapping his brain around her words. "You and I are chiefs and Jay's an Indian?" he asked. The silly metaphor is the only thing that came to mind.

She shrugged her shoulders. "I hadn't thought of it like that. I'm fire, you're water, by nature we're incompatible and… yeah, your analogy fits."

His brows furrowed. "I'm in, but how do you think he'll take it?"

She swished her lips. "I don't know. We haven't talked since Thanksgiving…" Her voice trailed off.

He grabbed her hips and lifted her upwards so their mouths were level. "I want you now. All your talk is making me hornier," he said in a husky voice filled with desire.

Within minutes, he was inside her, his jeans around his ankles and her sweats one leg in, one leg out as he thrust inside her, Eilida's back against the wall.

Breaking the News

Eilida snatched her mail out of the mailbox and flipped through it as she strolled back to her apartment. A square, cream envelope with no return address caught her eye. She lifted the glued flap and edged out the card inside it carefully. Stopping short of her door, she flipped the card open. It was an invitation to New Mexico. The familiar crop of horror settled into her soul. She stuffed it into its envelope and proceeded into her apartment.

Since she and Tommy came to an understanding about their relationship, he needed to know and she wouldn't be surprised if he got an invite too. He'd told her all about Scarlett and the money she'd paid him for the work he'd done living with Evan. It gave her chills to think of stepping into the monster's house and meeting his biological mother, yet it excited her too.

First, they were meeting with Burkhalder. She didn't have to talk him into it. He agreed right away, no coercion or trickery. If they were to keep things jovial between them, he understood he needed to agree to her requests and not lie. This made her something of an alpha, but he was far more alpha than she in bed.

That evening after class, Tommy picked up Eilida and they headed towards South Carolina to see her cop friend. He remembered her from the time she and her Tom Selleck look-a-like boyfriend visited Poppy Hills. As she climbed into the truck, he stole a glance. Her hair hung thick and bouncy across her chest, moving up and down against her perky breasts as she breathed. It took all he had to fight the hard on forming inside his pants.

The day unusually warm, she wore only a light hoodie, carrying a heavier thermal one on her arm which she pushed into the backseat.

"Hey," she said with a smile.

"You're not wearing a bra. How am I supposed to drive?" he asked, a smile painted on his lips.

"By watching the road, and I never wear bras unless my tops are thin." She chuckled.

Shifting into drive, he cruised out of the parking lot as she punched the address into the GPS.

He did his best to keep his eyes on the road instead of her breasts. The trees barren and the grass yellowish-brown, not much to look at now but in the spring, when all the flowers were in bloom and the leaves and buds burst forth on the trees, it was an amazing drive.

He pushed the button and the sunroof rolled back, allowing the warm air to soak them. It wasn't entirely unusual in the south to have a warm day or two splashed between the cold ones and he reveled in them when they happened.

Glancing at her, she had her tablet in her hands while reading a book. He cracked a smile and she caught it from her peripheral vision.

She tilted her head and peeled her eyes off the tablet. "I see you catching a glimpse."

He shrugged and reached for her leg. She covered his hand with hers. Their little come to terms moment and compromise was working well and she'd be all his later. He grimaced slightly at the idea of sharing her, then sucked it up. *Heck, it might turn me on more.*

A couple hours later, they pulled into the parking lot of a strip mall in coastal South Carolina. It had a variety of shops such as Violet's Chicken Garbanzo to Rockin' Reds Consignment. They walked towards Muggs Coffeehouse where they were meeting Burkhalder, the red-headed cop, and her boyfriend.

Inside, Kenny Chesney played through the speakers quietly to not limit conversation and the sensuous aroma of coffee filled his nostrils. He spotted her thick, red waves right away and the Tom Selleck look-a-like appeared the same. As he moved closer to the couple, he noticed more laugh lines around their eyes and a few more gray hairs on their heads. The couple sat on puffy green pleather chairs, a small table in front of them and two puffy green pleather chairs on the opposite side.

The Tom Selleck guy stood and offered his hand in a shake as Tommy approached him. "Frank Roy."

"Alice Burkhalder," said the red-headed woman who also stood, her arm in a sling.

He nodded. "I'm Dillon," he replied, shaking Frank's hand then Alice's.

Eilida gave Alice a hug then shook Frank's hand. "So nice to meet you," she said.

"The pleasure is mine," Frank replied, taking his seat.

Eilida sat on the puffy chair and Tommy went to the counter and ordered their coffees. He winced at how he'd introduced himself. Scarlett was the only person who called him that, everyone else knew him as Tommy, but this cop, according to Eilida, was present when he was born and helped save his life and that of his parents so he thought Dillon more appropriate.

With coffee in hand, he walked towards the group. Alice wore a quizzical look on her face, then spoke as he took a seat, "Dillon, I'm sure Eilida told you, but I remember the night of your birth, unfortunately it wasn't the best circumstances. How are your parents?"

He sighed. "They died in a plane crash when I was fifteen."

Her mouth formed an O. "I'm sorry to hear that. They were so proud of you that night, especially your father. He was absolutely enamored. Your mother was worried, but we saw them to safety. Such a beautiful couple they were."

The mention of his parents brought him full circle to the present and reminded him of how emotionally vulnerable he'd been when he met Scarlett, allowing her to slip her sharpened cat claws into him. He cringed then released. If it hadn't been for her, the relationship he and Eilida had may have never developed and they did get rid of Evan permanently. He didn't know who murdered him, but assumed the invitations he and Eilida received would reveal his killer.

Tommy didn't say much as everyone else chatted and made small talk. After a short while, Eilida told the couple all about her findings in the charts and how she got hold of the charts. Hearing it a second time, he still marveled at how all the charts exposed the events to extreme details such as the Mora murders in 1998. It pointed directly to a hidden agenda. The Moras weren't nice people. It also directed a jagged finger at child victims, not just the Mora children. A full investigation revealed the couple as kidnappers of young children they later sold on the black-market. A child, Tyrus Reed, escaped from their home the night of their deaths. It wasn't an accident. Evan saved the child's life. As malevolent as he was, there was a timid child inside him that sought to right the wrongs of cruel parents.

Alice's green eyes flashed towards Tommy, who sat silent in deep thought. "How did you get involved with Evan? I understand what Eilida explained in the charts, but how did it happen?"

He took in a large breath and released. "Several years ago, Evan killed my best friend and his family. I walked in as he was," it was always difficult for him to remember what he saw, "raping Mark's father's girlfriend. I didn't think, but reacted. A paperweight lay on the dresser beside me, so I grabbed it and hit him on the back of the head. He slumped forward and I ran as fast as I could until it sunk in. From out of nowhere, a lady appeared. Her eyes something from a mythical fantasy book, one green and the other amber. She wore a flowing, cream dress with pockets in the front, and boots. Her blond hair cascaded over her shoulders. I thought I was dreaming. None of it seemed real. Time stopped in that moment until she asked me to come with her. Over the next few years, she told me her story and connection to Evan O'Conner." Tommy took a breath and glanced at all three sets of eyes staring at him.

Burkhalder broke the momentary silence. "She's his biological mother."

Now Tommy wore a quizzical expression. "Yeah."

"I chased Evan from the night he came into my town, raped Gala, and slaughtered Eilida's family. The quest stopped the day we found him dead in that cabin in Salvation Cove." She heaved and lifted her latte.

"You saw him that day?" asked Eilida.

Burkhalder nodded.

Frank jumped into the conversation. "I followed Dillon," he shifted his gaze to the young man, "and Evan from the first crime scene at the Turnwells', unaware there was a crime scene, to the cabin in Salvation Cove. From there I called Alice and watched the two of you," he continued gazing at Tommy, "exit the vehicle and enter the cabin. No one ever exited the cabin. When Alice arrived, we moved in and found him dead."

"I was on my way to the Turnwells' house when he called, but never made it there because I turned my SUV around. We didn't know he'd killed them or that you were in trouble. Our goal was to stop Evan." Burkhalder sighed.

Tommy didn't have a clue so much had happened that day. *Who else was watching?*

Tommy blew a few loose strands of hair from his face. Evan's body wasn't reported that day. It wasn't for another couple days that his body was found. "You never reported it. Why are you telling us this?"

"Because I don't want to believe you did it. The night you were born, I was there. Jax and I worked with the doctor and nurse who birthed you to get you and your parents to safety. Revenge is a strong motive, but the question is, was your sense of vengeance strong enough to kill another human?" She dug her green eyes into his soul.

Eilida tensed with Burkhalder's words. A part of her didn't want to believe she'd slept with a killer. The other part of her thought killing Evan the monster made Tommy the sexiest man alive. In her heart, she knew he didn't do it.

All eyes on him. He knew they wanted to know how two men went into a cabin, one died and the other disappeared. Burkhalder was truthful with him. She admitted to her and Frank leaving Evan's dead body lying its own bloody puddle. He swallowed his nerves.

"We were in the cabin. Evan had a crush on me." His skin crawled with thousands of biting ants at the memory. "I knew that. My part of the plan was to seduce him and stick his own prepared needle into his neck. I did that and held him down as he attempted to throw me off him. But the more energy he exerted the faster the drugs pumped through his body, leaving him as defenseless as any of his victims. I took his knife, the very same knife he used on his family, and brought it to his neck but when I swiped it caught on the chain, baring the ring. Both fell onto the bed and I panicked the same way I did the day I walked in on him. I collected my stuff and met Scarlett in the car."

Eilida shifted her wide eyes from one person to the next. "No one has mentioned how my car made it there."

Tommy nodded and wrung his hands. Frank and Alice narrowed their eyes as they stared at him. He tugged at his chin. "While I lived with Evan, I broke into his room when he was away. I freaked out when I saw his maps, the charts, then the wall of toys from each girl." He choked back the bile, the same as he'd done the day he found the room. "I took a bunch of photos and left, careful not to touch anything else. Before

I closed the door, I realized photos weren't enough to frame a killer, so I stole into his restroom looking for DNA."

Eilida gasped and covered her mouth, as if she hadn't heard that part of the story before.

He nodded, ashamed that their frame up included Eilida and her car. "Scarlett planted the pubic hair and stole the car. She also called the police." He shifted his eyes downward, ashamed of hurting Eilida.

Uncovering her mouth, Eilida seemed to forget, or forgive, his indiscretion and asked, "How did you get that knife? It was never found."

Tommy nodded. "Scarlett stole it from the lawyer's house…"

They all sat quiet, absorbing his words.

"I believe you, kid, but we still don't know who killed him," piped in Frank.

Tommy shrugged.

"We have invitations for Poppy Hills next week, maybe we'll get answers," asserted Burkhalder.

"You too?" asked Eilida.

Their heads bobbed in unison.

"Scarlett tends to be very melodramatic sometimes." Tommy

grinned, knowing he was the only person present that knew her. If they did, they wouldn't question it. But he was curious about the huge *Evan Hater fanclub* meeting. *Does she know who killed him?*

Family Secrets

All members of Scarlett's dramatic *Clue* whodunit get-together stared at each other from around the room.

A tall man in a suit served them lemonade off a silver serving tray, then glided to a small table set in the corner and removed two silver lids from platters of food. One contained a fruit mixture of pineapples, oranges, and pomegranates. The other held tiny finger sandwiches. He half-bowed, waved his arm towards the food and disappeared.

A shapely woman walked down the large circular staircase. Her asymmetrical, lime dress flowing against each step behind her. She wore her blond hair in an updo, with a few loose curls and silver strap platforms on her feet. Typical Scarlett, thought Tommy, as she came to a stop at the bottom of the stairs, all eyes on her.

"I'm so glad everyone made it. I'm Scarlett. I hope you're comfortable. Larry makes such delicious snacks."

The room was so silent, if a feather hit the floor everyone would jump.

"I think you all know why you're here. Each one of you is connected to Evan, the last owner of this magnificent house. I'm connected, same as you." She sashayed towards the butler who handed her a lemonade.

Frank got to the point, already tired of her games. "Why exactly are we here?"

"Because you all should know the truth." She shot Tommy a glance. "Dillon — or is it Tommy you prefer to be called now?" her eyes, one green the other amber, shifted toward Tommy, "was the last known person to see Evan alive—"

Eilida shivered, then interrupted Scarlett's moment. "You killed him! It was you!" Eilida shot at Tommy.

She got right to the heart of their plan. Inside, Tommy laughed, outside he took a defensive stance. All eyes in the room on Tommy, who shot back, flames of fury bursting from his devilishly blue eyes, "I didn't FUCKING kill him, Eilida. How many times do I need to tell you that?! I didn't do it. I wanted to do it, I seduced him, my skin crawling with the touch of his skin beneath my fingers. I sucked down my own vomit! Then shot his own loaded tranquilizer into his neck and held the knife to his throat. Then I...

chickened out. I don't have what it takes to kill anyone, even a vile creature like Evan. I thought of all the lives he took, his shelf of souvenirs flashing through my mind, faces of nameless girls marched across my brain and still I couldn't do it." The flames in his eyes receded and he dropped his gaze to the ground.

Scarlett walked towards Eilida and took her hands. "Honey, he didn't do it. I did."

Eilida pulled her hands away from Scarlett and took a couple steps backwards towards Burkhalder. Scarlett searched the faces of everyone in the room; mouths dropped at her revelation. "I gave him life and I took it." Her eyes shifted to Burkhalder. "Before you have me arrested, you need to know the entire story. The best way to do that is to show you. Come with me."

Eilida moved closer to Burkhalder who took her hand and whispered into her ear, "Good job, honey."

Scarlett walked towards the patio door, her heels clicking across the marble floor echoed through the silence in the house. She slid the door open. "Please."

The group followed her outside, Eilida clutching Burkhalder's hand in a tight grip of fear. They walked past to the pool towards the garage. Eilida took notice of the expensive sports cars taking residence in the garage. Next, she opened a door and clicked on the light. The glow lit a stairway. Scarlett glided up the stairs, the lower part of her dress dragging on each step as she walked.

She had enlightened Tommy on pieces of the story, but even he didn't know what awaited them.

Eilida gulped, let go of Burkhalder's hand, as the stairway was only wide enough for one person at a time. She dropped to the back, Tommy behind Scarlett, Burkhalder and Frank behind him, and Eilida last.

Scarlett turned on another light, its glow illuminating a large room with dark, menacing corners. She continued towards one with a bulky object barely outlined in the shadows and halted.

Everyone stopped as they drew close to her and the object that was clearly seen now. An operating table. All eyes focused on it.

Scarlett cleared her throat. "This is where Evan was created." Silence filled the air. "My father, also Philmonia's, the woman you know as Evan's mother, was a rapist. I am a product of one of his victims. When I was a child, my mother gave me up and I bounced from one foster home to another until I met Philmonia. A sister, I was never skeptical of the blood bond because we looked like twins, except for our eyes. Hers were pure blue, like the sky. I was young and didn't know insanity and violence could be passed genetically and by circumstances, but I soon found out.

"You see, she propositioned me and asked if I'd come live with her and her husband in their fine house. The idea of being more than the poor little girl begat from rape and having an actual family — I swooned with the opportunity. She picked me up after school one day and brought me here to the house. They wined and dined me and showed me a bedroom made for a princess, with a canopy bed, beautiful antique furniture, and a closet filled with designer dresses. I was dumbfounded. Never in my life had I seen anything so fine or had anyone show me that much attention. It was after a few days that they drugged me at dinner. I woke up here on that chair." She pointed towards it. Cobwebs and dust covered it now, but not a soul in the room didn't see a teenage girl strapped to it.

She took a deep breath then continued. "My mouth gagged, Mr. O'Conner stood above me. A medical table filled with shiny instruments stood beside him and my sister. They had medical masks on their faces and wore scrubs. I tried to scream, but with a gagged mouth lost precious oxygen. They kept me drugged and between my few moments of consciousness I figured out what they were doing. For days they left me there, injecting my… injecting his sperm into me. He couldn't just rape me. He had to perform medical experiments on me! He made his fortune selling medical supplies and had some dark, sexual fantasy about inseminating a patient. I'd wake up and have lucid moments when I saw them having sex in front of me. She screamed 'Oh, Dr. O'Conner' during her orgasms."

Tears dropped from her eyes and rolled down her cheeks. Scarlett wiped them away, sniffled, and continued. "Once the sperm took, they brought me to the house and locked me in the dream room. It became the room nightmares were born in. They kept me there for the nine months of my pregnancy with Evan. He never stood a chance, as evil begets evil. I tried to miscarry him, beating my stomach. But he wouldn't come out."

She took a few moments to gather herself. Burkhalder stepped towards her and folded Scarlett into her arms.

"Thank you. I needed that. I've never told this whole story before, but I need to finish." She drew away from Burkhalder and finished her story. "For nine months, that human abomination grew inside me. The day I went into labor they put blue contacts in my eyes and carted me to the hospital. A doctor, a friend of Mr. O'Conner's, dealt with the birth. He didn't know I wasn't Philmonia and, with Mr. O'Conner in the room, I couldn't scream for help, I couldn't tell them I wasn't her and that this beast inside me was forced into me against my will."

Eilida dropped her head onto Tommy's chest, tears filling her eyes. "I'm sorry I thought it was you," she whispered. He wrapped his arms around her and held her tight.

Scarlett's voice cracking, she put an ending on her horrific story. "He took me home with the baby. I had to hold him in my arms but I wanted to throw him against the wall. A living, breathing icon of my torture. At that moment, I realized how my mother must have felt about me. I was the abomination she was forced to live with and couldn't. When we got home, Philmonia took the baby

and strapped a breast pump on me,
forcing me to pump milk. I felt like a
cow, but I didn't have to see the little
demon they made me carry and birth.
After a few days, they unlocked my room
and told me to leave. Mr. O'Conner
handed me a duffle bag, filled with large
bills. I grabbed the bag; money was the
least they owed me, but at least they
didn't kill me. I took it and ran, scared
but happy my life was spared. Years later,
I read the story of Philmonia's death in
the papers. I knew the demon spawn did
it. When he was released from Windy
Oaks, I followed him, at a distance."

She took a deep breath. "I never
got close enough to stop him. After
Tommy ran from the cabin, I wasn't
surprised. I slipped inside and finished
the deed. It was my burden, and I did it
with pleasure. The little beast I tried so
hard to miscarry laid on the bed a grown
man, face planted in the sheets. I grabbed
the knife, crusted with the blood of his
family, lifted his head and sliced his neck,
slow and deep. I watched his blood pool
on the bed. Satisfied, I left." She stopped.

"Where did you get the knife?"
Eilida lifted her head from Tommy's
chest and questioned, her voice shaking.

"From the man who stole it after
Evan killed my sister and her family —

Mr.Fritz. He had it hidden in his own house, underneath the stones in his fireplace."

That revelation rang bells inside Burkhalder. "And you used it to blackmail him."

She nodded. "I did. As Evan's only living relative, a DNA test to prove it, I walked into his office. The look in his eyes when I lifted my veil and he saw my face was priceless. His skin white as a ghost, he gasped. When I dropped the DNA test on his desk in front of him he gurgled and I thought he was going to have a heart attack. His eyes shot to the test. After a few minutes, he gained control of his faculties and dragged Evan's DNA test from his drawer and placed them side by side. I forced him to pull strings and give me the house and all Evan's assets. It was the least he could do after covering up a crime and killer for so long. So many lives lost, destroyed because of my sister, Mr. Fritz, Mr. O'Conner Senior." Her body involuntarily shuddered.

The silence in the room was finally interrupted by Burkhalder. "We are all victims." She glanced towards each person in the room. "I have plenty of connections and will have the chair tested for your DNA, along with the knife. If both come out positive for your DNA," her green eyes narrowed as she looked towards Scarlett, "and the DNA of your sister and her family, I will not have you arrested. I think we have all suffered enough and this brings me the closure I've sought for decades."

Resolved

Tommy cornered Scarlett by the pool. Her timeline didn't make sense. She didn't have the time to kill Evan and return to the car.

"Tommy," she said, putting a hand to her chest, startled.

"You've been a mother of sorts to me and I'm sorry for the way I've treated you." He wasn't sorry, not one bit. She used him.

Placing a hand on his shoulder she replied, "You mean a lot to me, but you're not here to apologize. You don't believe my story."

He sure as hell didn't, not all of it anyways, and he knew her well enough to stop his game now and be honest with her. Lifting her hand off his shoulder, he said, "We have history, some good, some not. I believe you know who killed him, but it wasn't you. I went straight to the car, so unless you have supernatural abilities…"

She chuckled, interrupting him, "You don't think I had time. You were so distraught and discombobulated when you got to the car I don't think you remember correctly."

He was an emotional wreck, but not so much he got confused and lost time. "No, you didn't kill him. Who did?" he demanded.

"Maybe we weren't the only ones who wanted him dead. Maybe there was a contract on his life," she said, her voice mocking and her eyes blazing into his.

He gazed away and watched the water sparkle under the moonlight. "Don't tell me, but I will find out." He glanced back at her and walked out of her life forever.

Eilida waited for Tommy against the side of the rental car. "How'd it go?" she asked.

He smiled. "About as well as I thought it would." He walked towards her, placing his hands against the top of the car. "We make a great team," he whispered as his lips grazed her ear.

She smiled. "We do."

"I don't care who killed him. I have you," he said, just before he slipped his tongue in her mouth.

Eilida sat beside Jay, apologizing for her indiscretion. "Tommy and I have a connection that I can't deny. It wasn't until I talked with Patrice Renard – the astrologer – that I understood our connection. And we're good friends, but my heart belongs to you." It would take a little work to get Jay on board, but she cared for them both and wanted both of the men in her life. Together they made it complete.

"I love you E. Damnit, don't you know that yet?" He let go of her hands and stood, not giving her a chance to speak. "You're always so skittish about relationships, I never said it until now. It took you two years to sleep overnight with me. Hell, there's nothing I wouldn't do to be with you. Yeah, OK, I was hurt a little, but more shocked to see another man with you." He flipped his brown hair across his head. "I know your sexual appetite and we took a break. I'm over my shock."

"You love me?" she asked, as if in surprise.

"Hell yes!" he responded, grabbing her hands again and pulling her upwards then towards him. "I want you always, no matter what that entails."

Dirty thoughts that floated through her head as the words dropped from his lips. Maybe, he wouldn't be so hard to convince. Their lips met and she thought, *what a lucky woman I am to have both these men in my life.*

Epilogue

Haldon, Devlin, and Jenson Kurl all turned their heads as the sound of an approaching airboat caught their attention. Devlin stood, offering his hand to Scarlett as she stepped onto the dock. He snaked his arm around her and kissed her lips. Taking his hand, they walked towards the other men and sat down beside them.

"It's all over boys. We're in the clear," she said, wrapping an arm around Devlin and another around Jenson. Tommy would search, but never uncover the government's involvement in Evan's death, nor would the government ever know Jenson killed his half-brother. The hit plan was executed perfectly. Tommy was the only wild card, because of his emotional side, but level-headed and in enough control he played his part well.

She smiled and rubbed the back of Jenson's head. "My strong son." She kissed his head.

Jenson smiled. Evan robbed him of a mother and running the blade along his older half-brother's neck had been easy. He felt no remorse for his actions, only pride.

Ten years in the future...

Tommy graduated with a bachelor's degree in criminal justice then transferred to FBI training. He now works as a profiler and maintains both a mutual work relationship and unique friendship with Eilida. Busy with his career, his relationship with her and Jay worked well. He was in charge of his career and gave in sexually, whereas she remained in charge of that aspect. He and Jay became friends.

Eilida finished and turned in her paper. Her professor was so impressed that, with her permission, he sent it to papers across the nation where it was subsequently published. It caught the attention of the public and, upon graduation, she was offered a job as an investigative journalist. She and Jay live together and remain childless, doting on her best friend Sage's daughter. They also enjoy visits from Tommy when he's in town. As each of Evan's child victims became old enough, Eilida took the time to meet and talk with each one. It helped her heal and in turn helped them heal.

Burkhalder and Frank married and officially retired. Now they travel the country in an RV, visiting their niece Talla and her family often. Burkhalder accepted Scarlett's confession when the DNA matched, and Scarlett agreed to turn in all the evidence against Evan that Tommy stole. Frank's connections eventually came through and he learned the truth about Evan's death. Happy with their lives, he willingly pushed it to the back of his mind as not important; after all, the end result, Evan O'Conner's death, was all his wife needed to put her hunt into the past.

Scarlett lives happily in New Mexico amongst, and unfazed by, Evan and Philmonia's ghosts. Devlin, retired from the Corp, spends most of his time with her. The DNA results came back corroborating her story and Tommy handed over all Evan's charts, maps, and souvenirs which she turned in to the local police saying she'd found them while cleaning the garage attic. She also set up a trust account for Erica Turnwell – her niece and final victim of Evan — using Evan's money.

Mr. Fritz sent all his money, except fifteen thousand cash, to an account in Belize where it was syphoned by a computer hacker. He was unaware until the cruise ship he was on ported in Cozumel and he didn't make it back to the ship on time, leaving him stranded and penniless. The fifteen thousand was on the ship in a safe. He was last seen wandering the beach, mumbling under his breath.

Evan burns in hell with Philmonia and Evan Senior for their crimes against humanity.

EVAN'S GIRLS SERIES BOOK 1 SCARLETT

Chapter 1
Pseudo

April, 1961. 5 years old

The sunny day carried a light April breeze as I jumped off the last step on the bus. No sign that the hot summer was approaching quickly. My blue apron skirt bounced with the spring in my step and my saddle shoes beat against the pavement as I ran towards my mommy waiting at the front door.

She leaned down, her skirt brushing the cement walkway and wrapped her arms around me. "Hi, baby."

"Hi, Mommy. Look what I made today," I said with pride, as I lifted a large purple paper butterfly from my backpack.

"Oh, isn't that beautiful?" she said with surprise in her voice. "Let's hang that in your room, shall we?"

"Yes, yes," I agreed and rushed toward my room. The white walls garnered many butterflies of every color and size. My twin bed had a lavender comforter covered with purple and white butterflies and lavender curtains hung across the windows. My room was a haven made of my favorite color – purple. I stood by the spot where I wanted Mommy to hang my new butterfly.

She entered the room, her yellow skirt flounced at her knees with each step she took. Her dark hair tied up in a ponytail and her bright brown eyes smiled at me. "This is where you want it?"

"Uh huh."

She took a thumbtack and pinned the butterfly to the spot I pointed. "There you are. We'll show Daddy when he gets home." Her smile large and full of love.

"OK," I said, bouncing into the kitchen for my after school snack.

The sun lowered in the sky and Daddy came home. As soon as I heard the door open, I rushed toward him and he scooped me into his thick arms, filled with tickling hair. "How was your day?" he asked, his hazel eyes beamed with joy and sparkled in the setting light of the sun. His blond hair slicked back against his oval head.

"Good. I want to show you what I made."

"I must see it," he said in mock surprise.

"Mommy hung it in my room."

He hoisted me over his head and sat me square on his shoulders as we headed down the hallway. He entered the room.

"Do you see it daddy?" I asked.

"No," he said, spinning around and making me dizzy. "Is it here?" he asked, stopping and pointing to an old butterfly.

I giggled. This was our routine. "No, Daddy."

He spun again and asked, then again before he settled on the new one.

"It's just gorgeous, almost as pretty as you – my little butterfly." He lowered me.

I smiled a partially toothless smile. "I love you, Daddy."

"I love you. Hmm… where is my other love?" he said, asking about Mommy.

"I think she's finishing dinner."

He widened his eyes. "Oh, let's sneak up on her," he said, tiptoeing down the hallway and placing a finger over his mouth.

I stifled a chuckle and followed on my tiptoes. We peeked around the corner and Mommy gazed our way. "Oh, what do we have here?" she said, her eyes wide as if in surprise.

I giggled and Daddy wrapped his arms around her, planting a kiss on her lips.

It was a Friday and Genevieve, our elderly neighbor, came over about seven p.m. as always so my parents could enjoy date night. I couldn't pronounce her name, so I called her Gen. She wore her white hair in a bun and had kind blue eyes.

When the bell rang, I rushed toward it and flung the door wide open. "Don't you look pretty," she said.

"Thank you," I answered, spinning in my purple nightgown.

"Genevieve, come in," voiced my Daddy.

She stepped inside and took a seat with me at the kitchen table. I had the cards already out and waiting. I so enjoyed Friday nights and our card games, which she usually let me win.

My parents kissed my head and walked out the door.

Gen's blue eyes gazed into mine. "One day you will do something great. Very few people have eyes like yours and they give you a special oomph that others don't have."

I smiled. Gen loved my eyes. One was green and the other amber. She and my parents agreed that I was something superior, like a fairy. They insisted my eyes gave me special powers.

After an hour of cards, Gen tucked me into bed. "Goodnight Scarlett," she whispered, planting a gentle kiss on my cheek.

I woke up hours later to a large commotion in the house and the sound of Gen crying. Scared and worried, thinking Gen was hurt, I jumped out of bed and scurried down the hallway, halting at the end of it. A police officer dressed in uniform sat beside Gen on the couch. She was OK, but where were my parents?

My heart thumped against my ribcage. Another officer walked into the house, his eyes rested on me.

"How are you?" asked the officer. His mustache moved up and down with the motions of his mouth. He steadily walked towards me as I backed down the hallway.

"I need you to come with me," he said, getting closer with his hand out. I gazed into his dark eyes. There was no sparkle inside them. My heart beat faster when he took another step. Remembering the games I played with Daddy, I side-stepped him. His hand grabbed for mine when I slid underneath his legs, ran as fast as my two small feet could carry me and jumped onto Gen's lap. Wrapping my arms around her neck, I clung for my life.

I don't know what scared me so much, but an ominous sensation entered my gut and I knew my life was about to change for the worst. I should have woken up to Mommy and Daddy giggling, not Gen's sobs and two unknown people in my house. They wore badges but, to me, they were strangers.

"Shhh… Scarlett," Gen soothed as I scrambled to plaster myself against her.

"She has to come with us," said the officer in a deep voice.

"She's a little girl and confused. I will go with her," Gen said, her arms wrapped around my trembling body.

"Suit yourself," the deep-voiced officer huffed.

"Where's Mommy and Daddy?" I whispered in Gen's ear.

"Oh, Scarlett. You sweet baby. Your mommy and daddy…" she choked back a sob, "they aren't coming home."

I traced the flowered pattern on the couch with my finger as her words sunk in. "Why not?" I asked, my brows furrowed.

"They've gone to heaven," Gen responded in a gentle voice as she caressed the back of my head.

I didn't really understand. "Without me?"

Gen took a deep breath. "Yes, but it wasn't their choice. Their time on Earth has passed, but you still have a job to do." She lifted the hair above my ear and whispered, "Remember, one day you will do something magnificent."

I leaned back, still planted on her lap and looked into her blue eyes. "Because my eyes give me special powers."

"Yes," she chuckled, "because of your eyes."

Hand in hand with Gen, I walked out of my home, never to return, and climbed into the back of the police car.

Chapter Two
Eye Opener

Two years later

I was placed into a home for abandoned and orphaned children. Gen visited every so often for two years then never returned. My heart broke, she was the light in my life, my reason for living. Every day my heart ached for my parents. They loved me and my memories of them are burned into my heart with love.

"Hey, funk eyes," quipped Michelle, "no one will ever want you with those funky eyes. You'll be an orphan forever." She stood in front of me with her legs forming a wide V, preventing me from swinging. Her brown hair hung like limp spaghetti. She was my age, but much larger than me.

I stared at her, trying to tap into the special powers that existed in my eyes. I imagined telekinetically flinging her backwards into the concrete school. Her broken body sliding against it and puddling on the cement playground. I understood full well my eyes didn't really have any special powers but I enjoyed pretending they did. "You're in my way," I said.

"Make me move," she grunted.

I would if I could. A kickball rolled beside us and she left her stance long enough to lean down and grab the ball. I pushed hard and forced the swing as high as I could make it go in the few seconds I had. It whooshed past her, knocking her to the ground.

"Funk eyes," she sneered, dusting the dirt from her dress.

Ignoring her comment, I continued pumping the swing for the rest of recess. Michelle wasn't the worst. I only had to see her at school. At the home, Dana made it her life's purpose to destroy me. Within the week, the home had taken in a few more children, placing Dana and I in the same room. It was small, with barely enough room for the two beds and one tall dresser.

"Catch," shouted Dana as she threw her backpack at me and slid onto the bench school bus seat beside me. The heavy bag felt as though it was loaded with bricks. I pushed it toward her. Since I had to share a room I had to put up with being her mental punching bag. But I had a plan to at least keep my peace with her. She deplored kitchen duty, so I volunteered to take her share of kitchen chores.

I loved the kitchen, but was sure not to tell her that. It was far better for her to think she had me under her thumb.

Dana's hefty bag took up the space between us on the bus and she sat with her legs in the aisle so she could talk with the other students. Everyone knew we were the orphan kids, but she played like she was something more and vied for popularity. She was pretty with her long, straight, dirty blond hair, oval face and deep blue almond-shaped eyes.

The bus rolled to a stop and Dana stood. "Can you get that?" she asked, pointing to her brick-laden backpack.

I smiled, stood, and hefted the bag over my shoulders. The bag hit her in the side, knocking her into the seat on the other side of the aisle.

Her blue eyes glared at me and shot bullets into mine. "Watch it!" she screamed.

I didn't say a word, certainly not an apology, after all, I meant to do it. She thought much of herself and I was a couple years younger and only weighed forty-five pounds, but I was smarter than her. I marched off the bus, one step behind her. She stopped abruptly and I almost fell backwards from the weight of her bag, but the boy behind me caught the bag, evenly distributing the weight so I caught my balance.

I went straight to the room and dropped her weapon of a backpack onto her bed, then jaunted straight to the kitchen. I loved it there, as we were the first to taste any treats. I wrapped the smallest apron around myself, it was a couple sizes too big so I had to wrap the strings all the way around and tie it in the front and the bottom hung just above my ankles.

Today's treat was homemade brownies and milk. I piled them onto a plate while Mario, another orphan, grabbed the milk and a stack of cups. I left the innermost brownies in the pan and winked at him. He winked in response as we carried the snack to the others in the dining hall.

Once we dropped it off and served the others, we ran-walked back to the kitchen for our brownies, the moistest in the pan.

Later that night after dinner and clean up, I sat with the others as we watched The Andy Griffith Show and took turns bathing. We didn't get baths nightly since there were only two bathrooms and a limited amount of hot water. The ladies put us on a schedule according to room assignment. Tonight was mine and Dana's night as well as a couple other kids.

Dana strolled out of the bathroom, after her fifteen minutes was up, with a brush in her hand. She slicked down her wet hair as she took a seat beside me. "Your turn," she smirked.

"Dana, no brushing in the family room," scolded Moira, one of the ladies who ran the place.

"Yes ma'am," she said, seething under her breath and following behind me as I entered the bedroom to grab my bundle of night clothes.

She dropped her brush onto the dresser which she'd taken over. I had nothing on top of it and only one drawer at the bottom to put my clothes in. I didn't have many materialistic items anyways, mostly I had memories of the butterflies on my wall and my two beautiful parents.

Not wanting to miss any more TV, Dana scurried out the door without saying a word. I headed towards the bathroom.

By the time I was finished it was bedtime and the ladies scuttled us into our rooms. They were always in such a rush for us to get into bed. It was a routine they never deviated from. Moira poked her head into the room. Seeing us both in bed, she closed the door and went onto the next room.

Dana turned towards me and I never slept with my back to her as I wanted to see the attack head on. She folded her pillow and curled her fingers around the edges of it. "I overheard the ladies talking and they said your parents hated you," she whispered.

I knew better. "Why would they say that?"

"Because it's true, dummy. All our parents hated us, except mine. They loved me," she said with a taut smile on her face.

"How do you know? You're here too."

She ignored my question. "Your daddy is in jail and your mommy gave you up."

That's ridiculous, my parents died, I thought — but didn't say it. Instead I asked the question again that she'd side-stepped. "What about your parents?"

Still ignoring my question, she rolled her eyes. "Your daddy hurt your mommy." She emphasized hurt and it stung deep in my soul.

I didn't know at seven what she meant and was tired. She was mean and ugly inside, so I shut my eyes.

"Your daddy hurt her and a bunch of other women, that's why he's in jail." The words rolled off her tongue with stingers attached.

I ignored her words and kept my eyes closed. That was the first I learned of my biological parents.

The following day was Saturday and I waited for Cat, the lady who worked in the kitchen directing and teaching us, to disappear for her afternoon walk. I gulped down a little lemonade to wet my throat that was parched from the anticipation of what I was about to do, then left the kitchen and padded down the hall. Making sure no one was around, I peeked my head around the corner of the door to their small office.

The kids were all outside playing a game and Cat was on her walk, easy peasy. I slid into the room and headed straight to the file cabinet. The ladies made sure we understood this room was off-limits, but since nobody ever attempted to get inside they'd grown lackadaisical about locking it.

I stood on my tiptoes and thumbed through the folders. Finding mine, I opened it. What I read brought tears to my eyes. Everything Dana said was true. A church lady dropped me off at the orphanage when I was a newborn. It said in bold letters she was a rape victim and wanted nothing to do with the child. My birth certificate was inside the file; Melissa Jones was listed as my mother. The family I'd always thought were my parents took me in at three months old. They filed for adoption when I was five, but the papers were never finalized because of their early deaths.

Tears dropped from my eyes and my nose grew hot and leaked. I swiped my face with the apron and stuck my folder into its rightful slot. Rape — that word didn't exist in my vocabulary. Edging close to the door, I leaned in and, hearing nothing but the vacant house, I went back to the files and found Dana's.

It turns out her mother had her out of wedlock and was forced by her family to give her up. I thumbed through until I found her birth certificate and it listed Sam Courier as her father. I knew that name, somewhere I'd heard it before.

A door slammed and brought my mind to the present, so I shoved her folder back into the cabinet and closed it.

Female voices and clicking on the floors moved closer to the office. Panicking, I slid underneath the large wooden desk and curled into a tiny ball.

"See you at dinner, Cat," said Moira, as she pushed open the office door and took a seat at the desk. Luckily, I was small and scrunched into the darkest corner. All I saw was her black heels as they tapped the floor to Chubby Checker on the radio.

What felt like hours went by and my bladder was near bursting. Clutching against myself, I fought the urge to pee all over myself. The glass of lemonade I stole before sneaking into the office was my penance for the wrongs I just committed. A drizzle of pee trickled over my fingers and I knew I couldn't hold it any more. I looked around and spotted a vent on the other side of Moira's legs but didn't know how to get there without bumping into at least her feet.

Over the sound of the radio, I heard Cat call, "Moira."

Moira scooted her chair back and stood, offering me the opening I was waiting for. With one hand squeezing my crotch, and my bladder muscles tensed to keep it in, I scooted with my back against the desk and wall to the vent then pushed aside my soaked panties. The pee burned as it streamed into the floor vent, a little splashing against my legs and the floor. I guessed the vent was for heat but that wouldn't be used in Albuquerque, New Mexico until sometime in the winter. My flood of urine would be dry by then, although it would probably cast an awful odor once used. I shrugged, unconcerned as I felt so much better.

Moira left the office with Cat and I climbed out from under the desk. My wet panties felt cold and gross against my crotch. Scurrying to the door, I peeked out. Moira and Cat went around the corner toward the front door. I heard it creak open then closed and I seized the opportunity to sneak to my room, hoping Dana wasn't there.

My lucky day, the room was vacant. Then I heard voices calling for me. My panties uncomfortable against me, I walked bowlegged and wanted to change but thought to wait. I figured they were looking for me since I'd been gone so long. Scooting into the tiny area between my bed and the wall I grabbed a Nancy Drew novel, The Secret of the Old Clock, and began reading. At seven, I read better than all the students in my class.

The door opened and Moira walked in. "Scarlett."

I cringed. "I'm here," I replied, waving my hand in the air.

"What are you doing? We've been calling you for several minutes now," she said with concern in her voice.

I stood, a dribble of pee from my panties ran down my left leg. "I'm sorry," I said, hanging my head. "I was really into my book and didn't hear." I placed the book atop my bed.

She sighed. "Scarlett, I should have known." She moved to the front of my bed where I was now in full view. "Did you have an accident?"

I peered down my apron, a large wet spot was at the end of it. I must have accidentally peed more than a trickle when I soaked my hands. I shook my head no and responded, "I snuck a glass of lemonade earlier and I must have spilled some on my dress." I didn't want her to know, worried that at some point when they turned on the heat and the smell took over the house that they'd know I was the culprit, meaning I'd been in the office.

"Well come on, let's get that off you."

"OK, Miss Moira." I walked closer to her and she moved back allowing me the room.

Her eyebrows made a V while her forehead wrinkled. "You don't need to lie."

What? How did she know? Then I saw the wet bubbles shining on the linoleum right below where my butt had been. I thought back and assumed the splashes were more than I thought too.

"Turn around." she demanded.

I did, reluctantly.

"The back of your dress has a wet spot, too."

I gulped. "I'm sorry. I guess it happened while I was reading. I didn't even know." I rested my face in my hands and cried.

"It's OK, honey, you're still a young girl and accidents happen. Right now we need to get these clothes off you and get you into something dry. And you need a bath."

After my bath, I washed my clothes and hung them to dry. I'd be the laughing stock, as everyone would know I peed myself. It was embarrassing, but at least no one knew the reason I peed myself.

In bed that night Dana teased, "Do you need diapers like a baby? Do you need a bottle too?"

I tried to ignore her but then she said, "The little bastard baby nobody wants is retarded and still pees herself. Wa Wa." Her mocking tone made all the anger inside me rise to the surface.

"I'm not a bastard baby! My parents adored me."

Her eyes widened. "What a big vocabulary you have. Tch." Then she turned over and went to sleep.

That night, I waited for her to start snoring then left the room and grabbed a small disposable cup from the bathroom. I filled it with cold water and went back to my room and held the cup below her fingertips, and lifted it slowly until her fingers dangled into the water and waited a few minutes.

She moved in her sleep, so I quickly drank the water as I'd made no plans on how to get rid of it and jumped onto my bed, stuffing the cup into my pillow case.

Dana continued to wiggle in her sleep then jumped out of bed. I kept my head buried in my pillow to stifle my laughter.

"What did you do?!" she shouted.

I turned and jumped in mock surprise. My eyes wide and mouth forming an O.

Within seconds Cat was at the door. "What's going on in here?" she demanded.

Dana looked at her then me and her face grew red. "I… my bed."

Cat's eyes moved across Dana's nightgown. "Dana, you are eleven years old!" she scolded, her hands on her hips.

"I didn't, it was Scarlett," she said, tears in her eyes.

"Scarlett did not pee your bed. Grab those sheets and get a clean nightgown. You will take a bath and make your bed with new sheets. First thing in the morning you'll wash them."

Dana harrumphed. "But…" Cat gave her the stink eye with one eyebrow raised and Dana shut her mouth and did as she was asked.

I curled back onto my side and didn't hide my smile as they headed out the door.

Chapter Three

Boiling Point

The next morning I woke early when Cat entered the room and woke Dana to wash her sheets. My head buried in the pillow, I didn't see her but felt knives stabbing my back from the insidious stare I'm sure she passed my way.

Once she left the room I dressed and went to the library. There was a thick dictionary in the center of it and I wanted to know what the word rape meant. It said: unlawful sexual penetration of the vaginal area, anus, mouth, or sexual organ. I spent time looking up all those words and was still lost as I was only seven. My best guess was it meant an act of violence.

My mind rolling with new vocabulary I sauntered to the kitchen. My face must have worn a curious look as Cat asked when I entered, "What's on your mind?"

"Nothing," I responded and skipped to the stool I used while working and jumped on. "What are we making for breakfast?" I had the menu memorized and knew every third Sunday of the month we had waffles, scrambled eggs, and sausage.

She smiled and slid over a dozen fresh eggs, milk, a large bowl, and a whisk. "Go ahead and get started on the eggs," she said, pouring a cup of waffle mix onto the griddle and pressing down the top. Within thirty minutes Mario joined us and we were serving breakfast.

Dana stared at me, hate filling her eyes. I smiled as I walked past her and skirted towards the kitchen to eat the special waffles Cat made for Mario and I that had extra fresh strawberries cut on top.

Dana's behavior and torture grew worse over the next few months. I did my best to ignore her until she went too far. It was my birthday and Cat knew how much I loved butterflies and purple. I'd grown to like her and we had many kitchen conversations in which I'd told her about my parents. Her smile always kind.

For our birthdays we always got something from the ladies and cupcakes. The evening of my eighth birthday —

Tuesday November 5th — all the children and ladies gathered around. Cat made me special cupcakes with purple frosting and a piece of Dubble Bubble gum on top. As the ritual demanded I sat at the head of the table for dinner and cupcakes. Dana sat at the end. She didn't look my way until I received my gift.

Carefully, I unwrapped the curly purple bow and laid the thin gift, a square lump on top upside down and slid my finger under the tape and peeled back the paper. My eyes widened when I saw the glittery purple butterflies. In excitement I forgot my manners and snatched the gift out of the paper. A notebook and crayons.

"So you can draw and write your own stories," said Cat, smiling.

I jumped off the chair and ran to her side. "Thank you," I beamed, hugging her then Moira.

That day I forgot all about Dana and drew the night away, creating a story about magical butterflies. In bed that night I felt Dana's eyes on me. When I glanced her way, they were filled with hate. It was my day so I ignored her and went to sleep.

Two days later I woke up to my notebook ripped into three chunks and my story ripped from the notebook and lying in pieces by my head. Tears burned in my eyes. I understand now that Dana was jealous. The ladies loved me and did something special but at the time anger brew inside me. Dana wasn't in the room but my shock and scream that I don't remember making alerted Moira.

She flew into the room and clutched me in her arms. "What's wron…" she began, then noticed the balled up papers and chunks of notebook. "I'm so sorry, honey."

Moira walked me to the kitchen. She glanced at Cat. "It looks like someone destroyed her gift and I have a good idea who. Please stay with her until I sort this out."

Cat nodded then looked at me. "How about we deviate from the menu and have crepes for breakfast?" She ran her palms across her apron.

I knew she offered since that was my favorite with blueberries. I shuddered, sniffed back my tears and said, "OK."

It didn't take Cat long to find Dana. She appeared at the doorway to kitchen. "Scarlett, honey, please come with me."

By this time Cat had me in a good mood and full of fresh fruit. I nodded and hopped off my stool.

Dana sat at the dining room table hanging her head.

"Dana, look at me," ordered Moira, folding her arms. Dana peered upward through her hair. "Sit up straight and look at me." Dana did as asked, her face now visibly red from crying. I hoped she'd gotten a good whipping from Moira but knew she didn't as the ladies didn't believe in physical harm. Instead they used their eyes and guilt.

"What you did was wrong. You owe Scarlett an apology." Her eyes bore into Dana's.

Dana turned, swallowed hard, then glared at me. There was no apology or sadness for me in her eyes. "I'm sorry," she said in a quiet voice.

"Scarlett, you may go back to the kitchen," said Moira.

"Thank you, Dana," I said, taking another glance at her before I scurried back to the kitchen.

All day Dana glared at me; a look of hate painted on her face. Luckily she was older and we didn't see each other much in school but on the bus and after school she stuck virtual blades into my soul over and over. I don't know what else Moira told her but knew it would mean more torture.

That afternoon, while I was reading another Nancy Drew novel in the library Jenny, one of the older girls, entered and cleaned the windows with a new cleaner. She placed it on the table and left the room for a minute. I took a sip of my water then got an idea. I chugged my water then set it beside the cleaner, unscrewed the top and poured a little inside my glass which I then took to the kitchen. Cat's back turned, I shoved it to the back underneath my station and scurried out of the room before Cat noticed I was there.

I showed at the kitchen to do my chores. While prepping foods I caught sight of an empty spice bottle in the trash. It was the right size to hold the window cleaner sample. With everyone preoccupied I grabbed the empty spice bottle, poured the cleaner into it, then closed the top and stuck it in the pocket of my oversized apron. I couldn't pour it into dinner because everyone might get sick or it would be too diluted to have much effect. So I waited for the opportunity.

It happened Saturday. I kept the cleaner with me at all times because I didn't want to miss the one opportunity I'd have. Dana brought a glass of milk to the living area with her then left. A few

other children were in the room but
playing a game so they didn't notice when
I dumped the entire sample of cleaner
into Dana's milk. I left the room before
Dana returned and rinsed the small bottle
then buried it in the kitchen trash.
Nobody was in the kitchen, so that part
was easy.

I walked through the living room
to get to the library and Dana was
drinking the milk. I felt a tinge of success.
But real happiness came a couple hours
later when she was doubled over in pain
and threw up. Immediately she was taken
to the infirmary where doctors and
nurses who donated their time
determined she had a virus since no one
else was ill.

That night, and the next few
while she was in the infirmary, I went to
sleep with a huge smile on my face until I
was given devastating news.

All Charts done by and
astrological readings done by:
Marcha Fox
B.S. Physics, Dipl. IAA
www.ValkyrieAstrology.com

Her books *Whobeda's Guide to Basic Astrology* and *Definitive Guide to Astrological Reports* can be found at Amazon as well as many of her other books.

Volume III Ruthless Storm Trilogy

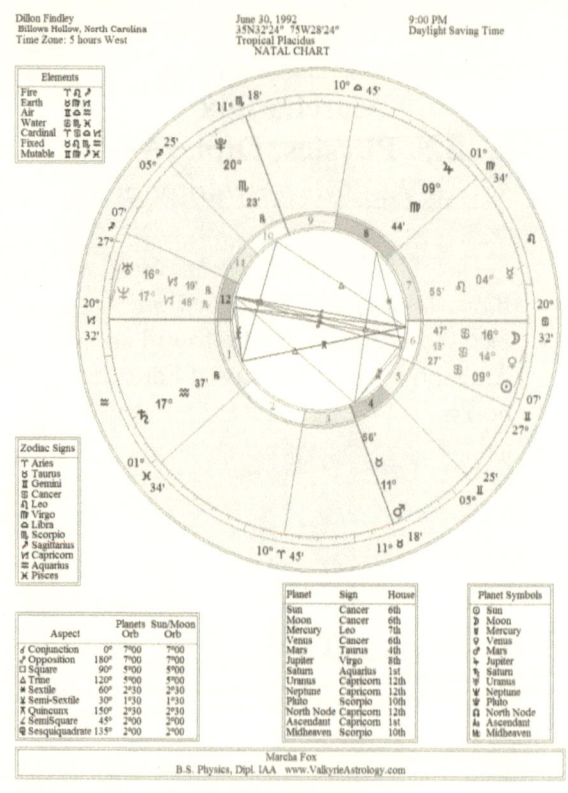

Dillon Findley
Billows Hollow, North Carolina
Time Zone: 5 hours West

June 30, 1992
35N32'24" 75W28'24"
Tropical Placidus
NATAL CHART

9:00 PM
Daylight Saving Time

Elements	
Fire	♈ ♌ ♐
Earth	♉ ♍ ♑
Air	♊ ♎ ♒
Water	♋ ♏ ♓
Cardinal	♈ ♋ ♎ ♑
Fixed	♉ ♌ ♏ ♒
Mutable	♊ ♍ ♐ ♓

Zodiac Signs	
♈	Aries
♉	Taurus
♊	Gemini
♋	Cancer
♌	Leo
♍	Virgo
♎	Libra
♏	Scorpio
♐	Sagittarius
♑	Capricorn
♒	Aquarius
♓	Pisces

Aspect		Planets Orb	Sun/Moon Orb
☌ Conjunction	0°	7°00	7°00
☍ Opposition	180°	7°00	7°00
□ Square	90°	5°00	5°00
△ Trine	120°	5°00	5°00
⚹ Sextile	60°	2°30	2°30
⚺ Semi-Sextile	30°	1°30	1°30
⚻ Quincunx	150°	2°30	2°30
∠ SemiSquare	45°	2°00	2°00
⚼ Sesquiquadrate	135°	2°00	2°00

Planet	Sign	House
Sun	Cancer	6th
Moon	Cancer	6th
Mercury	Leo	7th
Venus	Cancer	6th
Mars	Taurus	4th
Jupiter	Virgo	8th
Saturn	Aquarius	1st
Uranus	Capricorn	12th
Neptune	Capricorn	12th
Pluto	Scorpio	10th
North Node	Capricorn	12th
Ascendant	Capricorn	1st
Midheaven	Scorpio	10th

Planet Symbols	
☉	Sun
☽	Moon
☿	Mercury
♀	Venus
♂	Mars
♃	Jupiter
♄	Saturn
♅	Uranus
♆	Neptune
♇	Pluto
☊	North Node
Asc	Ascendant
Mc	Midheaven

Marcha Fox
B.S. Physics, Dipl. IAA   www.ValkyrieAstrology.com

The Cosmo Natal Report for

Dillon Findley
June 30, 1992
9:00 PM
Billows Hollow, North Carolina

Calculated for:
Daylight Savings Time,   Time Zone 5 hours
West
Latitude: 35 N 32 24   Longitude: 75 W 28 2
4

Positions of Planets at Birth:

Sun	9 Can 27	Pluto	20 Sco 23
Moon	16 Can 47	N. Node	0 Cap 42
Mercury	4 Leo 55	Asc.	20 Cap 32
Venus	14 Can 13	MC	11 Sco 18
Mars	11 Tau 56	2nd cusp	1 Pis 34
Jupiter	9 Vir 44	3rd cusp	10 Ari 45
Saturn	17 Aqu 37	5th cusp	5 Gem 25
Uranus	16 Cap 19	6th cusp	27 Gem 07
Neptune	17 Cap 48		

Chapter 1: How You Approach Life and How You Appear To Others

Capricorn Rising:

Cautious, prudent, and rather self-contained, you are a person who approaches life realistically and who is not inclined to take foolish chances or get carried away by the overly optimistic or idealistic schemes of starry-eyed dreamers. In fact, you frequently have a jaundiced view of such things. You are rather worldly-wise at a fairly young age, even something of a cynic. Often the world doesn't seem like a safe, friendly place to you, and you tend to approach life in a guarded, conservative manner. You are generally calculating and careful, and are rarely spontaneous, fluid, open, and childlike.

You are pragmatic, shrewd, and an excellent strategist, carefully planning your moves for maximum effectiveness and advantage. You are willing to work long and persistently for what you want and you often do things the hard way. You do not expect others to take care of you and sometimes refuse or simply don't seek any outside help. You are often very ambitious, but quietly so.

There is nothing flamboyant or flashy about your approach. You are very responsible, conscientious, and very concerned with your duties to others and how you appear in society, your "rank" so to speak.

To others you seem mature, serious, quiet, reflective, and emotionally detached. You dislike sloppy sentimentality and won't openly display your feelings, especially the softer ones. You like to always appear poised and in control and hate to show any weakness, vulnerability, or chinks in the armor.

You respect tradition and the time-honored way of doing things, and you feel there is much to be gained from studying history and also by learning from older, more experienced people. A wise mentor or father is often your guide in life, and you in turn develop a great deal of hard-earned wisdom which you like to impart to younger people.

You have a stern, authoritarian, no-nonsense aspect to your personality. You expect much from yourself and may not give yourself enough room to experiment and make mistakes.

You also tend to be rather close-fisted, to save and conserve your money and resources rather than spending, enjoying, or splurging with them. You spend money on things of quality and of lasting value, things which are good investments, but not frivolous, temporary pleasures. There is a bit of the ascetic in you. You have great self-discipline and self-control and can "do without" very well. Your tastes are generally understated and simple.

Though you may have other, more colorful and imaginative sides, the face you show the world is modest and rather conservative.

Neptune Conjunct Asc.:

You seem gentle and receptive and often you do not make a clear, strong impression on others. You have an elusive and subtle quality, and people may be nebulous about who you are. You are easily influenced by others and somewhat naive. You have a spiritual, mystical approach to life and are very idealistic and sometimes impractical.

Chapter 2: The Inner You: Your Real Motivation

Sun in Cancer:

You have powerful emotional attachments to the past, your family, your childhood, those places you associate with safety and security and your beginnings. Maintaining a connection with your roots and heritage and keeping family bonds strong are very important to you. Loyal, devoted, and sentimental, you tend to cling to whatever is dear to you, be it person, familiar place, or cherished possession.

You are sympathetic, nurturing, supportive, and very sensitive to the emotional needs of other people. You like to be needed, to care for others, and you often worry about the people you love. You have a very strong need for a sense of belonging and acceptance, and you center much of your life around your home. You are more concerned about people and their feelings than with power, achievement, or position in society. Kindness, consideration, and tenderness impress you more than any sort of honor the world can bestow.

322

You are primarily emotional and your views are often dominated by your feelings and by your own personal, subjective experiences, rather than reason, logic, or abstract principles. It is difficult for you to judge situations in a fair, objective manner for your personal sympathies and loyalties usually enter in. You take things very personally, and sometimes build a wall around yourself to protect yourself from pain and rejection. You feel rather shy and vulnerable at heart. You also tend to be moody, experiencing frequent emotional ups and downs. You need to have a place and time in your life to withdraw, introspect, dream, and replenish yourself; otherwise you become cranky and unhappy with those around you.

You function in an instinctive, nonrational manner and like to immerse yourself in creative activities where you can express your feelings, imagination, and instincts. You often love to cook, since it can be both creative and a way to nurture and nourish others. You also have a great affinity for music, because it evokes and communicates feelings that may be difficult or impossible to put into words.

Your compassion, sensitivity, and

imagination are your strong points. Your faults include an inability to release the past and go forward, clannishness and prejudice, and a tendency to be self-pitying when you meet hardships in life.

Sun in 6th house:

Your energies are directed to either perfecting your techniques, skills, and abilities in work, or in "perfecting", refining, and improving yourself as a person. Critical analysis and attention to minute detail are intrinsic in either process. The urge to bring about a state of wholeness or optimal functioning is a strong motivation of yours, and you are quite a perfectionist!

You can easily become overly identified or involved with the function you perform, with your work, or with your own health and "growth process".

Sun Conjunct Venus:

You are loving and well-loved by others, and have a strong need for kindness, friendship, and affection. Your artistic and creative powers are also well developed and you do everything in a harmonious, gracious, pleasing manner. Aesthetics are very important to you. Your personal appearance and attractiveness are also very important to you.

Sun Sextile Mars:

You are positive, vital, energetic, active, a go-getter. You enjoy competition, and your initiative and self-confidence make you a winner.

Sun Sextile Jupiter:

You have big aspirations but do not struggle or labor to achieve them. Your self-confidence and inner harmony attract success and benefits to you in an almost magical way. Your optimism and cheerful generosity also win you many allies and successes in life.

Chapter 3: Mental Interests and Abilities

Mercury in Leo:

You are a person of strong opinions and you express your views energetically and often dramatically. You are an entertaining speaker and will embellish or exaggerate in order to get your point across. You have an aptitude for story-telling and performing. Even if your arena is only the classroom or dining room table, you put on a good show. You have an abundance of creative ideas and do not enjoy a job in which you have no creative input or voice in decision-making. You could be a good politician, spokesperson, group leader, director, or coach.

Mercury in 7th house:

You are often involved in verbal exchanges, interviewing, discussing, debating, counseling, negotiating, getting and giving feedback, and sharing information. You are drawn to intelligent and verbal people, with whom you can communicate and from whom you can learn. You love to have an audience to hear your ideas, and you also appreciate eloquent presentations by others.

Chapter 4: Emotions: Moods, Feelings, Romance

Moon in Cancer:

You respond very much to the emotional tone and atmosphere around you, and can be dominated by your fluctuating and unpredictable moods. You often appear irrational to others because you cannot always explain the reason or source of your feelings. Anyone who lives with you must accept your ups and downs and appreciate your need for times of withdrawal.

You are also very sympathetic and understand the unspoken feelings and needs of others. You take slights and rebuffs very personally and though you may forgive a transgression by a friend or loved one, you never forget it.

Moon in 6th house:

You have a sympathetic nature and instinctively reach out to people in need of help. You also have a deeply ingrained tendency to want to improve or "fix" other people's lives, which can be annoying to the person who has no desire to be changed or "helped" in this way. For you, affection and caring must be expressed in tangible acts or service of some kind.

Moon Conjunct Venus:

No matter how you appear on the surface, you have a very soft heart and others can always appeal to your sympathetic, affectionate side. You especially care about the needs of children, mothers, and families, and you want a love partner who values marriage, home, and family as much as you do. Unkindness or harshness offends you very much.

Moon Opposition Uranus:

You crave excitement, change, and discovery, and cannot tolerate a routine or lifestyle that offers little in the way of surprise or challenge. Excitable, spontaneous, and enthusiastic about anything new, you may be perceived by others as being too impulsive, especially in personal relationships. It is not easy for you to make or keep commitments, since you don't know how you will be feeling from one day to the next. Emotional freedom is very important to you. Your domestic life can be very unstable - but you like it that way.

Moon Opposition Neptune:

You are a dreamer, attracted to the inner, mystical side of life, and may have trouble distinguishing the real from the imagined or illusory. You do not enjoy confrontation and become very evasive when problems in your personal life arise, escaping into your imagination in order to avoid dealing with them directly. You are also rather gullible and naive about people, especially if your sympathy has been aroused. You are very sensitive to music and can use it to bring yourself into emotional balance and harmony.

Moon Trine Pluto:

You enjoy emotional intensity and are attracted to the mysterious, the unknown, and to dangerous or challenging experiences which draw on all of your inner resources. You are able to handle an emotional crisis very well, and you are interested in the deep roots of emotional problems and how to cure them. You insist on bringing feelings between people out into the open, for you want real closeness and intimacy with others, without barriers or secrets.

Venus in Cancer:

Sensitive and sentimental, you are deeply attached to your family, old friends, familiar places, and the past. You are romantic and tender in love, and the remembrance of birthdays, anniversaries, family rituals, and other days of personal significance is very important to you. You seek caring, emotional support, and security in love. You like to be needed, to cherish and protect your loved ones, and you are somewhat possessive of them.

Venus in 6th house:

When you care about someone, you like to serve them, doing small thoughtful favors, helping them, or doing something tangible to show your affection.

You also have considerable artistic or creative skill and may sew or do other handiwork or crafts. In fact, you are suited for a profession involving beauty or pleasure or making people happy in some way.

Venus Opposition Uranus:

Your love feelings are easily aroused and your romantic relationships begin with a sudden electric attraction, but they often end abruptly, and you may be in and out of love frequently - especially in your younger years. You crave emotional excitement and need to feel spontaneous and free, so you may avoid making firm personal commitments. Unusual or nontraditional forms of love and relationships appeal to you, and you are attracted to unique, creative, or unstable people.

Venus Opposition Neptune:

You have a very romantic, idealistic vision of love and may be disillusioned to discover that no real, flesh-and-blood human being ever quite lives up to your dream image of the Perfect Love. Though you frequently fantasize about love and romance, you may avoid becoming intimately involved with anyone or making definite commitments. You can be evasive and dishonest with yourself and others, when it comes to love. Some of your love yearnings may be expressed through art, music, or an involvement with mysticism.

Venus Sextile Mars:

You are warmly romantic and openly express your appreciation and love of the opposite sex, though rarely in a crude or insensitive manner. You enjoy playing match-maker and bringing people together romantically. Fulfillment and harmony in love is likely for you because you know what you want and need in a romantic sense and express those desires honestly.

Chapter 5: Drive and Ambition: How You Achieve Your Goals

Mars in Taurus:

Once you set your mind on a goal, your dedication, determination, and commitment to it are extraordinary. You pursue your ambitions tenaciously and will stubbornly refuse to give up, let go, or be influenced in any way. Like Aesop's tortoise, you labor patiently and steadfastly until you achieve what you want - or until it is clear beyond a shadow of a doubt that all is lost. You are a reliable, consistent, and productive worker, and often shoulder more of the workload than your co- workers, usually without complaint. The nitty-gritty work often falls to you. You prefer a regular routine, with definite hours and clearly defined responsibilities and tasks. In fact, establishing a pattern or routine is very important to your success because once you get started in a certain direction, is easy for you to follow it through to its completion. Getting started is more difficult. You have a lazy, comfort-loving side and there is often a good deal of inertia for you to overcome before you get going. Once you get a momentum going, your energy level is strong and steady.

You are interested in concrete results and solid, practical achievement. You need to have some tangible product or contribution to show for your efforts, and cannot be content with only intangible rewards (such as having a good time, learning, or spiritual enrichment). Material well-being and security is also a large factor in determining what you do. Your stamina and persistence is your great strength but it can also work against you; you can get caught in a rut and refuse to seize new opportunities. You also tend to play it safe, and to limit yourself in that way.

Mars in 4th house:

It is not easy for you to show the world at large your angry or competitive side, but your family sees this side of you more often. Temper tantrums, tumultuous family relationships, or a great deal of competition between you and one or more of your relations is likely. You like to be the one in charge in your home and you put a lot of energy into making it the way you want it.

Mars Trine Jupiter:

Your self-confidence and vitality are strong and you believe you can do just about anything you want to. You have an enterprising spirit, a good sense of timing, and the ability to sense what will succeed and what won't. You usually make fortunate decisions in work or business activities. You enjoy healthy competition and you have a rather playful, good-humored attitude toward it. You mostly compete with yourself to see how far you can go or how much you can accomplish. You like to keep stretching your limits.

Mars Trine Uranus:

You are dynamic, decisive, and somewhat impulsive. You respond quickly and spontaneously to challenges, and you enjoy vigorous physical activities that require fast reflexes and a good sense of rhythm and timing. You have an abundance of energy and vitality, and a restless desire to see progress and change - you hate stagnation. You are individualistic and make a good leader, spearheading new projects and inspiring others to act.

Chapter 6: Other Influences

Jupiter in Virgo:

Your ability to think things through clearly, and to analyze and understand the smallest details of any plan, is highly developed. You have a modest nature and are more concerned with the success of your project or work than with personal aggrandizement. You enjoy working and are happiest when you are being productive and using your time efficiently.

Jupiter in 8th house:

You are successful in dealing with other people's money or material assets, either through your work or by combining and sharing what you have with someone else (marriage or business partner). An "inheritance" (either material or psychological) which comes through your spouse or other close partner is likely to benefit you immensely.

Saturn in Aquarius:

You have an innate distrust of groups and/or a cynical attitude toward society that may leave you feeling out of step and unable

337

to participate in activities with your peers. Overcoming a sense of aloofness and alienation from others is an important task for you.

Saturn in 1st house:

You have a mature, disciplined, serious attitude toward life which colors everything you do. Caution and realism are your virtues though you limit yourself at times by being too careful, shy, or fearful, and not believing in yourself enough or being assertive when necessary. Others find you difficult to get to know intimately, as you tend to distance yourself from them or to put forth a rather stern, "adult" face to the world.

Saturn Square Pluto:

Once you decide what you want to do, you will pursue it tenaciously and, if necessary, sacrifice a great deal for your deeply felt convictions. This trait tends to make you feel a little out of step with others. You take things a little more seriously and have an inclination to be a bit of a fanatic, although probably not flamboyantly so, so others may not know how deeply you feel and how driven you are about the things that are important to you. You have a deep inner resolve and are willing to struggle to do the things that are really meaningful to you, rather than follow an easier but less meaningful course in life.

Uranus in Capricorn:

You are part of a 7 year group of people who are active in reforming businesses, governments, and other large social structures. A great deal of streamlining and reorganizing takes place, most of which will help to improve the well-being of people, the ultimate goal of these reforms. Your generation will promote various reforms that will vary in different nations. For example, some will increase socialization of public services and others will put more services in the hands of private industry. In either case, your generation strives for greater efficiency and a great deal of waste is eliminated from industry and government.

Uranus in 12th house:

Most people do not see your wild, daring, "crazy" side, and you yourself may be unaware of it! You tend to hold back the unconventional, inventive, impulsive side of you nature - or to live it out only in your private fantasies. You may have strange dreams!

Uranus Conjunct Neptune:

You were also born during a period that
lasted approximately 5 years and is
characterized by an unusually high degree of
imagination and sensitivity. You are part of
a group of people who are very inspired but
also unstable. Many unusual contributions to
the arts, music, religion, and psychic
development are brought forth from your
age group. These works are often strange
and bizarre, and always original. Your age
group also inspires intense political
movements that are often fanatical or
unreasonable in their goals.

Neptune in Capricorn:

You are part of a 14 year group of people
who are conservative and traditional in
spiritual aspirations and religious outlook.
Your age group returns to some traditional
basics in religion, and also traditional styles
in music and art. Classical music and
literature have a revival with your age
group, and a great deal of inspiration is
gained from the masters of arts, music,
literature, and philosophy throughout

history. Your age group is contemplative and reflective about religious matters and you take an objective and logical approach to religious issues. Many of you are cynics and critics of spiritual and metaphysical ideas.

Other age groups criticize your group for not having enough heart and compassion. Sometimes this is true and is evidenced by some unusually crafty and manipulative fraud and deception that occurs in the higher ranks of governments and large businesses.

Neptune in 12th house:

Compassionate and extremely sensitive to the emotional tones in the atmosphere surrounding you, you are naturally "psychic" or able to sense and understand much about a person without talking to them or knowing them consciously at all. You are deeply interested in the hidden realms of life and the afterlife. Your powerful sensitivity may also remain latent or repressed through much of your life and then be fully awakened in adulthood.

Neptune Sextile Pluto:

The entire generation to which you

belong has tremendous opportunities for spiritual rebirth and awakening. This will not be forced upon you or precipitated by unavoidable events, rather it comes from an inner yearning and a natural propensity to seek the depths.

Pluto in Scorpio:

You are part of a 12 year group of people who have a complex and deep emotional side. Your age group has a great fascination for the mysteries of life, and members of your age group will make extraordinary breakthroughs in the understanding of life processes; major advances in biological sciences will open up new technological possibilities. Intensive probing into genetic structure and cellular processes will accelerate genetic engineering into new vistas. Your generation also probes the mysteries of birth and death, and members of your age group will even develop laboratories for forging new understanding of what happens at birth and death. Other breakthroughs will be made in the understanding of animal behavior and sexual activity. Archeological studies will unearth vast new insights into the history of man, and the exploration of the ocean will receive a new impetus, spurred by unusual and interesting findings made at the bottom of the sea.

Behind all of this work is the deep, probing, penetrating interest in the mysterious. There is a deep fascination with sex, power, and the occult as well. Hypnosis, karate, and other mental and physical training techniques are likely to be very popular with your age group. The love of mystery is also likely to bring a revival of mystery novels and movies; your age group will bring the macabre into current fashion and style.

You are an emotionally complex group, and you can be prone to some very strange behavior. Intrigue and mystery are exciting to your age group, and hopefully this does not get the better of you, causing you to act in a cruel or grotesque manner. There is a chance that crime, violence, and emotional disturbance will be relatively high in your age group, but hopefully your interest in the mysterious, strange, grotesque, and macabre will not manifest in this way.

Pluto in 10th house:

You have a powerful sense of destiny and may be unusually, even ruthlessly, ambitious. There is a very driven, compulsive quality to the way you pursue your career or other important life goals, which is likely to win you both staunch admirers and vigorous opponents.

There is a very "radical" side to you, and you may want to remake or change the world in some significant way. Depending on other astrological factors in your chart and your own decisions, you can be either very destructive or a powerful force for healing and positive change in the world.

www.ingramcontent.com/pod-product-compliance
Lightning Source LLC
Chambersburg PA
CBHW032234010726
47494CB00002B/483